ALSO BY ROBERT POYTON

INNSMOUTH ECHOES

THE DUNWICH TRILOGY
THE DUNWICH NIGHTMARE

THE WOLF WHO WOULD BE KING SERIES
WOLF IN SHADOWS

THIS IS AN INNSMOUTH GOLD BOOK

ISBN: 978-0-9956454-2-4

Copyright@ 2017 R Poyton.

Published by Cutting Edge on behalf of Innsmouth Gold.

www.innsmouthgold.com

REMNANTS

Tales of Fenland Horrors & Hauntings

Robert C Poyton

From R. To L.
Queen of all my Dreams

CONTENTS

FOREWORD

There are three major influences on this collection of stories. The first two are literary; the authors MR James and HP Lovecraft. The third is geographical, the East Anglia Fens.

MR James (1862–1936) is known as the father of the English ghost story, and with good reason. There can be few people in the UK who have not read one of his stories or seen a TV adaptation. Indeed, it is a tradition to have an MR James adaptation on Christmas television, echoing James' own Yuletide ghost readings. James was provost of King's College, Cambridge from 1905 to 1918 and many of his stories are set in East Anglia. James moved the ghost story away from gothic cliché into a more contemporary setting. His protagonists tend to be bookish types who discover that curiosity is not just fatal for felines. If you would like to know more about James, I recommend the excellent *Podcast to the Curious* at www.mrjamespodcast.com. Also, try and see the performances of Robert Lloyd Parry, whose live readings of MRJ are a delight. www.nunkie.co.uk.

HP Lovecraft (1890–1937) is possibly the most influential author in the field of horror and even science fiction. Primarily a writer for pulp magazines, such as *Weird Tales*, he is best known today for his *Cthulhu Mythos*. Lovecraft also moved beyond typical gothic settings, inventing a whole new genre that continues to inspire writers to this day. Lovecraft was a native of Providence, New England, and many of his stories are also set in a particular locale - the places themselves almost form another character in the story. For more information on Lovecraft, I would direct to the reader to the most informative and entertaining *HP Lovecraft Literary Podcast* at www.hppodcraft.com.

Which brings me to my third influence - the East Anglia Fens. I moved from East London up to the Fens in the Nineties and it was quite a culture shock! The first thing you notice is the landscape, of course. Beyond that, you discover a rich history; Iron Age settlements, Hereward the Wake, the Middle Ages (when the region teemed with trade), the great draining of the fens and beyond. Small wonder, then, that the area is rich in folklore and ghost stories. The landscape itself has a haunting quality and there are numerous old ruins and picturesque villages to explore.

It seemed only natural, then, to use East Anglia as a setting for these stories - after all, it was good enough for James! I also think there are strong links between Lovecraft's New England and James' East Anglia; indeed, many places share names, architectural styles and atmospheres.

For part of my research I read many books on local history and would like, in particular, to mention Richard Watson's excellent *The Lost Treasure of King John: The Fenland's Greatest Mystery*. Every school kid knows King John lost the Crown Jewels in The Wash, but I never knew there was such an interesting back story to the whole event; the Barons' rebellion, Magna Carta, foreign invasions, scheming monks, blackmail and possibly murder - if no one has made a film of this yet, they should!

So here, then, are thirteen stories, an affectionate homage to MRJ, HPL and Fenland lore. I've had a lot of fun writing them and I hope you enjoy reading them. In closing, I'd just like to mention that I have taken numerous liberties with place names and these events are all based on imagination and myth. And remember, there are no such thing as ghosts... until you meet one.

RCP
Jan 2017

REMNANTS

I could see the old church spire from my back window, up on the hill there. Well, what passes for a hill round here. Let's face it, a bump in the ground or a molehill counts in these parts, being as flat as it is. Nonetheless, All Saints was up on the top of a kind of ridge and one afternoon I thought I'd go up and have a look.

I've not been long in the village. I'm in one of those new bungalows on the edge, the new estate. Well, since Trish has gone I don't need much space. There's just me and Jess now. Jess came with me of course. Border collie she is, we're both knocking on a bit, but there's some life left in us yet.

So off we trundled, up Chapel Hill, then there's a turning into Church Lane. Not much more than a single track really, there's a couple of houses on the corner then, at the very end of the lane, we came to the church. Now I'm not one for architecture and I couldn't tell you a thing about churches, but it was a pleasant enough building. There was a notice board on the side, with service times and the like and something of the church history. Built in the 12th century, originally called St Margaret's, knocked about a bit by Cromwell and his lads, then smartened up a bit in the mid 1800s. In 1900 it seems the spire was struck by lightning and the place wasn't fully restored until the 1920s.

It's nice to know a bit of local history and I would've had a look inside, but the place was closed up. Reckon that's how they have to be these days. So I took to having a walk round the graveyard. Not a big place, but then it's not a big village and you could see the same local names cropping up over again. At the back there was a small gate in the wall and a track leading off along the ridge. Having nothing better to do, I thought we'd take a walk along it.

It was quite a view from up there – the fields stretched away on both sides, you could see across to Tydd St Giles to the north and Gorefield to the south. A distant tractor toiled slowly across the landscape, followed by seagulls. It reminded me of one of those toy farm sets we used to have as kids. Anyway, it was a nice day, a bit blowy, but it usually is out this way. Jess was running around in circles as collies are want to do.

Up ahead, at the end of the track, was a clump of trees that I thought would make a good turning round point. When we got there though, I found the trees weren't wild woodland, but were well ordered. I found myself in what looked like an old, overgrown orchard. There was a small path, also overgrown, that I followed and, after a couple of minutes I came to a line of trees that screened an enclosed area.

There was no building here now but it was obvious there had been at some time. You could see the outline of what I guessed was a cottage of some sort. No walls left, just low, moss and ivy-covered brickwork a foot or so high. I moved in for a closer look, prodding round here and there with my stick.

Sheltered from the wind, the surrounding trees put the whole area in shade and I shivered a touch from the drop in temperature. Standing at what I guessed was the front of the property, I could make out the edge of the building and see an overgrown garden of some sort at the back. I walked through the "front door". I know it sounds a bit silly but I did say; "hello is anyone in?"

Well it seemed like the polite thing to do. There was some brickwork and rubble underfoot, all covered by untold years of vegetation.

It was then that something caught my eye. As I said, at the back of the place was an overgrown garden. A flash of white caught my attention. Jess was busy on the scent of something – rabbits, I imagine. I carefully picked my way across the house and out the back. There it was again, that flash of white. Stepping out of the house I found myself in what was once, I'm guessing, a fruit garden or allotment. Blackberry bushes grew high and I had to push my way through. There was the white flash again. At the back of the garden was an untidy hedge with a waist high wooden gate. Caught in the hedge, flapping, was a large piece of plastic sheet. Blown in from the farmland, no doubt, it rustled loudly in the wind, waving and popping as though trying to escape.

I let out a breath – I didn't even realise I had been holding it. I suddenly realised how, except for the snapping of the sheet, it was deathly quiet here. I had a sudden sense of isolation. It occurred to me that there was no other living soul around me for at least half a mile in each direction. It's quite a strange feeling to have, in what some people regard as a small, crowded country. It was then that a faint smell of jasmine came to me. The odour snagged a memory somewhere at the back of my mind. It reminded me of Trish's favourite perfume, I always used to buy it for her at Christams - *Shalimar* it was called, I used to tease her about the name. Here, though, for some reason I found the smell disturbing, it felt out of place and my happy memory felt unwelcome.

I pushed my way back through the brambles and called to Jess. Within minutes, we were back through the orchard and out into the open. It was like coming out into the modern world again, back into the present. Even the distant tractor felt like a link to humanity.

It was on the next visit that I first saw her. That wasn't until a couple of weeks later. There was a funeral up at the church, my next-door-but-one neighbour. I hadn't really known him that well, just chatted a couple of times - but it seemed the right thing to do. Places like this are close-knit and it doesn't do to be stand-offish. Anyway, after the service and burial people were milling round as they do. I didn't fancy going back to his house for the wake, not really knowing any of the family. It was then that the gate at the back of the churchyard caught my eye and I wondered about that old house. Maybe I was testing myself – I'd spooked myself a bit last time. Perhaps I thought I had something to prove. Perhaps it was some kind of curiosity that drew me.

In any case, ten minutes later I was once again winding my way through the small orchard to the front of the plot. This time I rooted around a bit more in the rubble. I wondered if there might be some clue to the former residents, but there was nothing to speak of. I did find some remnants of furniture, what looked like a chair leg, a couple of pieces of old cutlery, a broken picture frame, some fragments of china, but nothing more.

I pushed once more through the brambles at the rear. The plastic sheeting was gone, presumably off to haunt another hedge. I looked around the rest of the garden. There were the remains of a shed off to one side, completely overgrown, the roof sagging. I again noticed the stillness, the absence of any birdsong and once more that faint smell of jasmine.
When I looked back to the gate in the hedge she was there. Silent. A young woman in her twenties, wearing a white dress. She was staring at me impassively.

The surprise of it actually made me stagger back. In fact, I
tripped and fell, landing on my backside with a thump. When
I got up she was gone. I rushed over to the gate. It took some
opening but with a couple of bangs, I got the latch undone
and went through. There was a narrow earthen path on the
other side of the hedge leading off to the right. With the
hedge on one side and trees on the other, it seemed there
was nowhere else for a person to go, yet the path was empty.
I went along the path for about twenty paces, my heart
racing. I suppose she could have run off, but why would
someone do that? I headed back to the gate and noticed that
faint, lingering smell of jasmine. Shutting the gate behind me,
I hurried once again through the house, through the orchard
and out into the open, where I breathed deeply once more.

The next day, chaos descended when David and Melissa
arrived with the twins. It was the first time that my son and
his wife had been to the new place and the kids were all over
it of course. The adults were off on a long weekend break,
driving up to the Lake District, and I agreed to have the girls
for a couple of days. It would make a nice change to have a lot
of noise and activity going on and of course Jess loves the
twins. That took my mind off things I suppose, squeals and
laughter, the occasional crash as some ornament or other
went for a burton. I didn't mind really, kids will be kids. It
was nice too that they could play outside here with no
worries. The open space must have seen amazing to them,
living in a flat in town as they do.

So everything was fine until the last night. I was tucking the
kids in and had just finished their story about ten little
rubber ducks.

"There now", I said, "time for sleepy-byes".

It was little Sophie who said it, "Grandpa, can I ask a question?"

"Course you can, poppet," I answered

"Why is the lady so sad?"

I felt a chill on my spine. "What lady is that, sweetheart?"

"The lady in the garden, Grandpa. She is ever so sad."

My heart was pounding, but I had to stay calm for the kids.

"Don't you worry about her, Sophie, she is alright. You think about those little ducks, alright? Quack quack quack!"

I mimed flapping wings and they both giggled. I dimmed the light and left the room, going straight to the drinks cabinet and pouring myself a large scotch. Jess laid her head on my leg and I ruffled her fur. "Well old girl, what do you make of that?"

David and Melissa were back the following morning, and after lunch I waved them all off. The place suddenly seemed very empty and quiet. Early evening I made my way down to the local pub, the wonderfully named Woadsmans Arms. I'd been in a few times since moving in, usually for Sunday lunch. The place was warm and inviting and it seemed the same regulars were in the same spot whatever time you went in.

A couple of them nodded to me and I ordered a pint from Jake, the young manager. As he handed me my change I asked him

"So Jake, that old place up at the back of the church. Do you know anything about it?"

Jake shook his head.

"No good asking him," smiled one of the regulars, Mark, a young farmer. "He's only been here five minutes, he's a new boy!" The rest of the group chuckled and Jake rolled his eyes, smiling.

"You see how it is," he said, "I've been here ten years but I'm still the new boy!"

"Why do you ask?" Mark nodded to me.

"I just wondered. I was up there walking the dog the other week. Seems odd, place all knocked down and that."

"I don't really know to be honest." Mark continued, "I think it was a farm cottage There's an old orchard up there right? Maybe it burnt down or something."

"Didn't burn down, boy, it was knocked down!" came a voice from the corner, it was one of the old farm hands.

"There you go," said Mark. "Old Stan'll tell you all the gossip. He's lived here since the Middle Ages!"
The group laughed again. Stan took a sip of his Guinness and tilted back his cap with stiff fingers, revealing a brown weather- beaten face.

"You young boys don't know nothing," he tutted. "Place was knocked down by the farmer what owned it. My old man told me about it. Was around or just after the war – the first one. His daughter was living there with her young man. They'd just got married, then he was called off to France. He never came back. Anyway, the daughter lived there for a while, then disappeared, it seems. So the father had the place demolished. We were told not to go up there as kids. We did once though, a group of us."
We all awaited the next part of the story, but Stan drained his glass and set it down with a thump.

"Well I'll be off then, must crack on!" and with that he left the pub.

What set my mind on going up to the old house again? I think it was the perfume. That's the trouble with smells, especially faint ones. You are not sure if you are imagining them or not. But I woke up once or twice in the middle of the night, certain that I could smell jasmine. Not that I went up to the ruin the next day. No, it took me a couple of days to convince myself that there must be some rational explanation. Just a chance glimpse of some rambler or hiker. The jasmine... well that was just imagination and remembering Trish. The loneliness of the place, combined with a memory, to produce a sensation, that was all it was.

So it wasn't until the Friday afternoon that I found myself up at the church again. I went through the back gate and let Jess off the lead. She immediately went charging off, nose to the ground, bum in the air, in that funny dog way. Through the orchard and to the front of the house. I don't mind admitting my heart was already racing and my mouth dry. Once again I picked my way through the remains of the house and pushed through the brambles at the back. Nothing was there, just the empty silence. Jess, nosing around at my feet, managed to get tangled in the briars. I knelt down to free her, stabbing myself on a thorn as I did so. Sucking the blood from my thumb, I glanced up.

There she was again. Standing at the gate, just looking. The wave of loneliness hit me harder this time, almost like a physical blow. I blinked for a second and she was gone. This time, I ran to the gate and pushed through. Stepping onto the path I thought I glimpsed a wisp of white ahead. I ran along the path, breathing heavily, pushing undergrowth aside with my stick.

The trees and hedge suddenly gave way and I found myself in a small clearing. Ahead was a large, circular, stagnant pool, it looked man- made. Most of the surface was covered in vivid green algae. There was heavy smell of rot in the air and a slight hint of jasmine. The surrounding trees leant over the pond, everything was wild and overgrown. The place was dark, cold and damp. There was no sign of the woman.

I walked slowly towards the pool. Where I could see it, the water looked dark and forbidding, weeds waving just below the surface. Once more I noticed the absence of sound. No wind stirred the trees, there was no bird song, not even the hum of insects you would expect around a still pond.

I looked out over the water and as I watched, a languid ripple spread towards me from the centre of the pond. Then I saw her again. Out near the centre, the algae seemed to part and she was there, below the water. Arms outstretched. The sleeves of her white dress billowing softly. Her face pale and cold, eyes closed. Long, floating hair weaved with weeds. Suddenly, her eyes opened and she looked directly at me. All at once I felt the full pain of her loss. I experienced her sorrow, understood her grief... the long years of waiting, the empty loneliness....

It was Jess that saved me. She was stood on the bank barking furiously at me, that's what snapped me around, brought me back to the present. With horror, I realised I was up to my chest in the water. Flinching, I reeled back, the foul algae clinging to my clothes. I turned and splashed hurriedly back to the bank, clambering out. My legs were soaked and dark with mud, weeds clung to me, the rank odour was overpowering.

I don't remember much else until I got home, only a sobbing half-run, half-stumble back to the churchyard. Jess led the way. I can only hope none of the neighbours saw me, most likely they would all have been out at work. Once home, I binned my clothes and spent a long time in the shower before sitting down with another large scotch. Jess

17

got a special treat that night, the steak I was saving for the weekend!

There's not much more to tell. I had a word with a few of the local farmers and the vicar. By and by, with a little persuasion, I managed to get a small group up at the pond with some dredging equipment. It's common enough round here, what with all the dykes. I had expressed concern of how dangerous the deep pond could be if any local kids went up there. Maybe they bought it, but I saw a few exchanged glances from some of the old boys.

I was there when they found her. Once they cleaned the black slime and weeds away there wasn't much left. Just some bones wearing a simple wedding dress... a veil covering a once joyful face, hands clasping a long rotted bouquet, a ring glinting on a bony finger. Sad remnants of what was the happiest day of her life.

I have to say the old farmers were very respectful with the remains. She was placed gently onto a tarpaulin and someone called for the vicar. Considered opinion was that she had thrown herself into the pond. She knew her man was never coming back, so you could say she died of a broken heart. I suppose in those days that sort of thing was hushed up; in his shame and grief the father just demolished the place. Well, you can't imagine him wanting to live there again can you?

About a week later, after the police had been in and checked everything over, I was at the church again for another funeral. There wasn't such a big turn out this time, just me and Jess, the vicar and a couple of the younger farmers. I know the church used to be strict about this sort of thing, but the Vicar is a good fellow and thought the poor girl deserved the peace of consecrated ground.

It was as we stood there at the end of the service, her remains being lowered into a small plot, that I smelt it again. The scent of jasmine, very strong..... then as the sun broke through the clouds, it faded away on the soft breeze.

CAXTON GIBBET

Take an exit off the busy A428 at Caxton Roundabout, turn onto one of the smaller side roads and you will soon be in a landscape unchanged for generations. Of course, you can see the new development on the horizon and the gentle whisper of traffic is ever-present, but Eastern Brook flows lazily through the surrounding fields as it always has. And there is still a dirt track alongside the brook leading from here to there.

In the height of summer, the crops grow tall and the poppies and cornflowers bend gracefully over the edge of the track. Take a moment to enjoy the lazy hum of bees and feel the sun-warmed earth under a cloudless powder-blue sky; the peace and solitude is timeless.

On such a day as this, some three hundred years ago, the peace is broken by a lumbering figure in a great hurry. As he comes along the brook path, he is muttering under his breath and lashing out at the vegetation with his heavy stick.

Jack Williamson is a heavyset man in his thirties. His ruddy face and plain, coarse clothing mark him as a farm labourer, though his true calling is poaching. Locals are used to seeing his brindle lurcher, Flash, at his master's heels, but on this day Jack is unaccompanied... and angry. No, he is beyond angry. He is furious, incandescent with rage and grief! For Flash, his pride and joy, is no more.

The dog was forever with him, a faithful companion. At night, they roam the wide Cambridgeshire fields together, hunting any and all kind of game. Since the Black Act was passed, poaching has become more challenging, but Jack is a master of his illicit trade and Flash has earned his reputation as the best hunting dog in the county.

You might almost say that the dog is the love of Jack's life and his long-suffering wife, Ellen, would bitterly agree. Jack has never raised his stick, let alone his voice, to the dog but does not show the same courtesy to his wife. Things being as they are divorce is not an option for Ellen Williamson and so she bears her station with as much dignity as she can muster. She takes the beatings and her husband's other clumsy, drunken attentions with resignation.

But now the loyal Flash is dead! The once hale and hearty dog sickened for many days and, earlier this morning, passed away. Deafened by shock and anguish. Jack disregards his wife's expressions of sympathy and lets forth a stream of foul curses.

"I know just who did this," he rants at her. "That Albert Partridge, damn his eyes! Everyone knows he's jealous of my Flash! That dog of his is useless. Flash would best him in everything. He's faster, more reliable, braver ... yes, it's him what's done this and I means to have it out with him!"

With that, he pushes Ellen aside and, taking the heavy holly staff from its hook behind the back door, thunders out of their small cottage.

The bright, sunny day does nothing to lighten Jack's mood. If anything, his darkness grows with every pounding step, the lack of Flash at his heel a constant reminder of his loss. Reaching the edge of the field, he turns the corner only to see Albert Partridge, the source of his misery, strolling towards him without a care in the world!

"Morning, Jack," Albert calls with a grin. "What's about ye?" Face contorted in anger, Jack confronts his enemy.

"Why you!" Jack sputters in rage and raises his arm, cracking Albert such a blow to the head that he falls straight to the ground. Three times the heavy stick rises and falls. Then, stillness descends once more on the summer field, save for the harsh sound of Jack's laboured breathing.

With a final oath and a savage kick to Albert's lifeless body, Jack strides off in the direction of Caxton village. Later, at the Red Lion inn, Jack is well into his cups when some of his cronies arrive.

"You look happy, bor, been rabbiting?" asks One-Eyed Sam.

"Oh, no," Jack lets out a humourless laugh,"but I got a partridge ... a big 'un, too."

"Did the gamekeeper not see thee?" Sly Tom enquires. Jack takes a long draught from his earthenware mug and glowers at his companions over its rim.

"Ain't no gamekeeper to watch that partridge!" he snarls. The men, accustomed to Jack's dark moods, withdraw to another corner of the room, leaving him to his solitary drinking.

Of course, Albert Partridge's body is presently found and village gossip being what it is, soon turns to Jack's drunken mutterings. Two constables are dispatched to the Williamson's cottage. Jack laughs in their faces, saying "You won't find no partridge feathers here!"

Even when taken before the local magistrate, Jack continues his mocking tone. The blood-stained stick proves to be the damning factor in his guilt. It was brought forth by Seth Pryor, the Williamson's handsome, young neighbour. He had found it hanging on its hook behind the cottage door, still stained with the blood of its victim.

The case goes up to county court and there can be only one sentence for such a crime. The judge duly places the black cap on his head and intones: "Jack Williamson, you will be taken hence to the prison in which you were last confined and, from there, to a place of execution..."

The sentence is the gibbet. On many occasions, the accused is hanged by the neck until dead and then the body placed in the gibbet to serve as a stark, gruesome warning to others. This is not one of those occasions.

So it comes to pass that, on a cold and miserable December morning, Jack is placed in the iron cage which, in turn, is suspended from Caxton Gibbet, almost within sight of the scene of the crime. Only at this point, it seems, does Jack finally realise the true nature of his fate.

Those who gathered to watch later report the man's wild "loud and aggravated ravings". He calls for his dog, Flash, even for his wife, Ellen, and finally falls to cursing his own fate and all those around him.

Jack is left to die, of exposure to the wintry elements or hunger or thirst – whichever will take him first. His ravings continue and locals begin to hurry past the gibbet, eyes averted and ears closed, eventually bypassing the area altogether. Coachmen whip their horses harder and hurriedly drive their horrified passengers past. Even the morbidly curious tire of the spectacle and no longer visit.

And so Jack is abandoned to his torment, with no one to listen to his outbursts, other than the occasional patient crow. There is one final visitor, however, who arrives unnoticed now that Jack no longer draws a crowd.

Jack does not have long left on this earth. The discomfort is indescribable. Parts of the iron cage dig into soft flesh. Other parts of his body are numbed by the icy chill, the tears of self-pity frozen on his cheeks. The cold contrasts with the burning thirst. Biting hunger pangs wrack his stomach.

A gentle cough makes Jack open his gritted eyes... he can barely make out the figure below, gazing up at him. Slowly, he realises it is Ellen. Has she come to deliver him from this hellish place? Is his she to be his angel of mercy?

Ellen pulls the fur collar of her smart, new cape up around her ears. She digs into a pocket and pulls out a small blue, stoppered bottle. She holds it up briefly for Jack to see. Removing the cork, she slowly tips the bottle and ground glass pours out, to be blown away by the Fenland wind. Ellen throws the bottle aside, gives Jack a final withering look , the traces of a smile playing on her face. Then, without a word, she turns her back and walks away. Jack's final shriek carries across the grey, flat countryside, then fades into nothingness.

Caxton Gibbet is no longer near the old junction where the ancient coach roads met. It now stands not far away, at the entrance to a fast food restaurant. It is still the original gallows, though. Of course, it has a new beam and the post had to be replaced at some point - the hook, too. But it's still the original gallows.

If you go back to the crossroads and search around you will find a small mound where the gibbet used to stand. And if you linger there on certain winter nights, you may well hear, carried on the cold, lazy wind, the distant shriek of a dying and desperate man.

COBWEBS & DUST

"The greatest force is derived from the power of thought.
The universe is a cobweb; minds are spiders."
- Swami Vivekananda

L ethbridge waits until the group is assembled then, closing the heavy door, takes position by the desk. "What is it, I wonder," he asks, "that makes a man run howling from a building to his doom?" He pauses, taking another draw on his cigarette.

"And not from some gothic mansion or haunted castle on a storm-ravaged night. No, this was from a room in a library... in fact, the very room in which we are now gathered!"

The group shifts impatiently. Dean Heywood glances at his pocket watch. The cadaverous Head Porter Dollond tugs on his ear and stares fixedly at a point on the wall.

"And it is because of what happened then, and subsequent events, that I now strongly advise this room be sealed." Lethbridge seats himself on the edge of the large desk.

The room in question is a library. The simple plaque on the door proclaims it the *Manby Rare Books Room*. On entering the room you first see, to your left, the desk on which Lethbridge currently sits. Behind the desk, the room's large, sole window looks out onto a quadrangle. To the right, on either side of a central aisle, several large, dark, old, empty bookcases stretch away into the gloom.

The jowled, bespectacled Vice Chancellor Beaumont is the first of the group to speak.
"Come, come, Lethbridge, surely what happened then was just an accident; why should this be of concern to us now?"

"Ah well," Lethbridge stubs out his cigarette in the ash tray on the desk, "some *nows* are connected with particularly germane *thens* and it may well be prudent to be cognizant of those connections. I have pieced together as best I can, from Parker's own notes and from various lines of enquiry, what I believe to be the facts of the case. But, please, won't you be seated gentlemen? "

"Will this take long?" enquires the bird-like Reverend Lowe. "Only I have evensong to attend presently."

"Not to worry Reverend, we will be finished before it gets... dark."

The group shuffles, chairs scrape on the wooden floor and soon all are seated. Proctor Barcroft takes the opportunity to have a quick nip from his hip flask. Lethbridge remains still as an owl, perched on the edge of the desk. The only sound is the dry ticking of a clock. Then Lethbridge clears his throat and begins.

"I believe it started with a visit to Cecil Court in London. Did you know that Cecil Court was the first address of Mozart when he was in England?"

Dean Heywood sighs loudly and rolls his eyes.

"Ah yes, well in any case, as I'm sure you are aware, Cecil Court is home to numerous antique book shops. It was here, I think, that Parker first became aware of the actual location of the book. He had seen mentions of it, rumours, hints of hints, legend and lore of course, but nothing substantial - until he found that reference in Cecil Court.

But I must tell you something of Parker, of course, some of you may not have met him. He was in his first year of studies in the Philosophy of Religion. He was not a large man, quite short of stature in fact, dark of hair, somewhat saturnine in appearance. Always impeccably dressed, that is what most people remember of him. That and his eyes - bright blue eyes with a piercing gaze. He was quite an intense young man. I met him twice, once in a professional capacity here at the college, and once at a lecture on Yoga by Crowley.

Parker had a great interest in the darker areas of occult lore. Whether he was a practitioner of those dark arts we cannot say, though certain items found in his lodgings would strongly indicate an involvement that went beyond the casual. Much of his spare time, according to acquaintances, was spent in researching and collecting rare occult works. He was a regular at Deighton Bell and other such establishments. I have gathered there was one book especially that became a particular obsession of his, a book entitled *Liber de Portae Octo Baal*.

So, to return to Cecil Court, it was in June last year that Parker visited a certain bookshop there. The proprietor, Geoffrey Watkins, told me what happened..."

◆

The bell over the door tinkled and Watkins looked up from his newspaper. A short, well dressed man entered and nodded to the bookstore owner. Watkins nodded back.

"Good morning sir. If there is anything I can help you with please let me know."

The man grunted in reply and began browsing. He quickly moved past the newer books to the antique collection at the rear of the shop. He fingered various tomes, glanced through a couple more, then turned to Watkins.

"I'm looking specifically for rare occult texts - antique, not the modern kind of populist rubbish!" he snapped.
Watkins forced a strained smile. "Of course sir. Well if there is nothing that interests you here, I have some newly arrived items that have not yet gone out on display. If you would like

to come through to the back room?"

Watkins led the way through a curtained doorway into the musty stock room. He gestured to the collection of boxes and books on the tables. "Please, feel free to look through, I will be out front if you need me."

Parker began rummaging through the boxes. Many of them were old and dusty and as he lifted one, a large spider ran across his hand. Parker flinched, flicking his hand to rid himself of the beast. Most of the books he quickly discarded. Three he placed to one side, though on closer inspection they proved to be not of interest. He was about to pass back through the curtain, when a slim yellow volume caught his eye. It had been concealed down the side of one of the boxes.

Drawing it out he saw it was a German title, *Der Schwarze Spiegel*. Opening, he saw that is was printed in Dusseldorf in 1837. The title of the book stirred some memory from his previous research and he began leafing through the yellowed pages. His German was very poor, so he could determine very little of the text's meaning, but one repeated phrase stood out as if in bold print... *Liber de Portae Octo Baal*! Now this was a find indeed! He carried the book through to the counter.

"I am interested in this book, how much is it please?" Watkins examined the book and thought for a minute.

"Well, it's quite a rarity, a history of certain aspects of demonology, very few were ever printed. Three guineas." Parker grimaced. "I'm afraid that is beyond my current means. Is there any room for negotiation?"

Something about Parker's character irritated Watkins, the air of arrogance perhaps. So he made a quick decision.

"I'm afraid not, three guineas is the asking price." Parker sighed, "Very well, I will replace the book in its box."

He returned to the back room and was halfway through

replacing the book in the box when a thought occurred. He glanced around at the other titles, picking up and moving several until he found what he was looking for - a book around the same size as the one he desired. Swiftly, he removed the fly covering from the newer book and wrapped it around the German title. He returned once again to the counter.

"I think I will take this one please, how much is it?" Watkins glanced up at the proffered book.

"Umm... The Tarot of the Bohemians? Ten shillings please."

Parker hastily handed over the money, tucked the receipt into the book and, refusing the offer of wrapping or bag, quickly left the store.

The next week was spent in translating his new acquisition, with the assistance of a student in the Faculty of Modern Languages. Through the information gained, Parker was able to pull together a number of threads and, after consulting various other references and asking questions of certain people, came to his conclusion... the University Library had a copy of *Liber de Portae Octo Baal.*

◆

"And what is so special about this Porto Octo whatsit?" asks the Vice Chancellor. Lethbridge lights another cigarette before continuing.

"Those of you acquainted with such things will have heard, perhaps, of *Liber de Portae Octo Baal,* or *The Eight Gates of Baal.* First published in 1664 it is probably the rarest manual of demonology. Most works on witchcraft were written by inquisitors, but here is a book written by a genuine occultist, Olaus van Laar. A 'known trafficker with the Dark Powers,' it is written. As the first book ever to defend witches, it was almost immediately sentenced to the flames by the Inquisition and, it is said, only two copies remain. "

The Reverend interjects. "Indeed, this book has an evil reputation. I believe Waite described it as 'one of the most atrocious of its class'. It's considered highly dangerous by all accounts. One can imagine the allure of such a title to a person like Parker!"

Lethbridge nods, glancing at the clock and the lengthening shadows in the quad.

"And is there a copy of this book in our library?" asks the Dean, "and if so, what does it have to do with Parker's accident?"

"If I may continue gentlemen, I trust all will become clear." Lethbridge settles on the uncomfortable desk edge once more.

"Following this revelation, Parker began to devote all his efforts to tracking down the grimoire. Now, while the library system at the University is one of the finest in the world, it is also one of the largest collections, spread across many different locations. Despite his best efforts, Parker could find no trace of the book. Until fortune - or perhaps misfortune - smiled on him. It so happens that the sister of one of Parker's fellow lodgers holds a position in the library - in fact at this very desk; one Miss Margaret King. This room, as I'm sure you are aware, door, is a repository of many of the University's rarest tomes and incunabula. As such, access is strictly monitored, by Miss King, in fact written permission from the authorities is required to view certain books.

Parker reasoned that any forbidden titles may well rest within these walls... and he was right. This was not something he found out a first, I might add. No, for many weeks he courted young Miss King and was, by all accounts, quite the gallant. To cut to the chase gentlemen, Parker eventually gained access to this room via his wooing of Miss King. That he had any intention of honouring his promises to Miss King I severely doubt. In any case, he is beyond such promises now...."

◆

Parker virtually skipped up the entrance steps and pushed through the large doors of the library building. He wasted no glance at the porter behind the desk, or the busts and other pieces of art in the lobby, but headed straight for the large stone staircase at the side of the hall. Taking the steps two at a time, he was soon hurrying along the first floor corridor, his heels echoing behind him. Coming to the first door on the right, he knocked and entered the room. Margaret sat at the large desk, framed by the light streaming in through the window behind her.

"Hello darling!" he smiled, his heart pounding.

"Why Walter, what a pleasant surprise!" Margaret rose and came around the desk, giving him a peck on the cheek. She removed her spectacles and indicated the room with a wave of her hand.

"Well this is it, my domain!"

"It looks wonderful - mind if I have a look round?"

"No you go ahead, I have to finish this cataloguing. But please don't touch anything, darling and if anyone comes in - well, let me deal with that."

Parker squeezed her hands and immediately began prowling the rows of bookcases, like a predator stalking its prey. Nothing... nothing... nothing! With increasing impatience he continued his way down the aisle, exploring the stacks on each side. As he reached the last row Parker growled in frustration - still nothing! Then he noticed the door set at the back of the room. He grasped the knob and slowly turned it - locked! Parker gritted his teeth and thought for a moment, then returned to the desk. As he went back up the aisle his face transformed from scowl to smile.

"Find anything interesting?" Margaret smiled up at him.

"Not really darling. What's that door at the end though, what does that lead to?"

"Oh, that's where the rarest books are kept. Would you like to see?"

"Only if you are not too busy, darling." Parker maintained a calm exterior but inside he was raging. Margaret took a ring of keys from the desk drawer and Parker followed her back down the aisle. She unlocked the door and the two of them stepped into a small room lined with shelves. Parker's eyes darted hither and thither, hungrily roaming over the antique books and manuscripts. Then he saw it - in the corner sat a dark, wood chest. As casually as possible he asked, "what's in there?"

"Ah, *The Eight Gates,* it's a very rare title on demonology. It's on the prohibited list, like all of the books in here. You need written permission to view any of them. "

Parker feigned disinterest, then made a show of looking at his watch. "Oh sorry darling, I must go - just remembered I'm supposed to be at a lecture in ten minutes!"

With a peck on the cheek Parker left the room and exited the building. His mind was aflame with desire for the book, tempered with the circumstances of its storage. As he walked away from the old building, he noticed a small gaggle of local urchins, sat on a wall, jeering at passing students. A plan began to take shape in his mind.

Late the next afternoon, Margaret was clearing away in

preparation for going home, when there was a knock and a young boy's head appeared around the library door.

"Miss, miss, come quick, there's been an accident!" he blurted out.

"An accident, whatever do you mean?" Margaret rose.

"Quick miss, please! It's an emergelency!"

The head disappeared and Margaret went to the door. The boy was already at the far end of the corridor beckoning to her. "It's down here, miss!"

The boy moved off and she followed, turning the corner at the end and moving deeper into the old building.

Swiftly and silently, Parker moved from his position at the stair end of the corridor and entered the library. A moment's rummaging in the drawer, then he strode to the store room door and unlocked it. His hands were trembling slightly as he moved to the chest and opened the creaking lid. Inside, wrapped in black cloth, was a locked, iron box with an inscription stamped into the lid. Parker checked the key ring and, finding a small key, unlocked the box, opened the lid and gasped in triumph at what lay within. Full calf binding, gilt spine, red label... *Liber de Portae Octo Baal!*

He carefully removed the book, brushing the cobwebs and dust from it, putting it in the leather satchel he had brought with him. He then locked the iron box, wrapped it back in the black cloth and returned it to the chest.

Swiftly locking the storeroom door, he returned the keys to the desk, then moved to the main door, peering out into the corridor. As he did so he had the obscure notion of a vague sigh behind him and the faint odour of burning paper.

Disregarding both, he retreated quickly along the corridor and back down the stairs, the satchel under his arm. Nodding to the porter at the reception desk, within seconds he was through the doors and back out into the busy Cambridge streets. Margaret meanwhile, having lost the small boy in the labyrinth of corridors, returned to her desk, somewhat bemused. She tidied up her things, locked up, and set off for home.

◆

"It is at this point that tracing the course of events became somewhat difficult," Lethbridge continues. "For, of course, the very essence of Parker's enterprise was secrecy. But I did find and follow some threads which helped unravel Parker's activities. Two people at Parker's lodgings have been most helpful; the cleaning lady, Mrs Earnshaw and Parker's fellow lodger Noel King, brother of Margaret. King took some finding, but I eventually traced him to The Globe Inn Hotel at Burnstow, on the coast. He told me he was staying there in order to recuperate from... well that will become clear presently. In any case, I was able to meet King and discover his role in the events surrounding Parker."

◆

Noel King sighed and turned once more in his bed. For the third night running, his upstairs neighbour, Parker, was pacing about and muttering. His heavy footsteps and sonorous voice echoed through the old house, making it very difficult to sleep. Eventually, King reached breaking point. Putting on his gown and slippers, he strode out of his room and up the stairs, where he banged on Parker's door.

The noise inside stopped. After a short delay, the door opened slightly and Parker thrust his head through the gap.

"What?" he demanded.

"Come on Parker, old man, it's two in the morning and this is the third night you've been making this infernal row! Have some consideration, some of us are studying for exams, don't you know!"

"Exams!" snarled Parker. "Tests set by idiots, for morons! I'm in pursuit of true knowledge here, go away King and stop interrupting me!" He made to shut the door but King inserted a slippered foot into the gap.

"Now look here, you simply can't continue with all this racket! And there's no need to get insulting, Parker, just have some thought for others! Speaking of which, Margaret was asking why you haven't spoken to her this past few days?"

"Margaret, what do I care for Margaret? Why don't you and your drab of a sister just leave me alone!"

Parker had opened the door more fully now and King caught a glimpse of the candle-lit room, the rug rolled back and a lectern with a book on it in the centre of the floor. Then Parker moved forward, pushing him on the chest. The insult to his sister and the physical contact were the last straw for King.

"Why, you rotter!" he exclaimed and hit Parker squarely on the nose.

Parker was knocked back into the room. His blue eyes blazed with malice, his face contorted in fury. In the dim light he reminded King of a squat, mediaeval gargoyle come to hideous life. Blood dripped slowly from his nose to the floor. Parker made no move however, he merely hissed between gritted teeth. "You'll pay for that King.... just you see... you will pay!"

There was a soft plop as blood dripped from Parker's nose to the floorboard. Parker raised a hand to his face, then examined his red fingers. His snarl was replaced by a look of dawning comprehension.

"Blood... of course! Blood!" He cackled and with that, slammed the door in King's face.

The next evening began quietly enough and King presumed that his intervention had ensured a restful night's sleep. As it transpired, the events of that night led to King having no restful sleep for some considerable time thereafter.

He had retired at the normal time and, having had a late meal and a number of glasses of port, fell quickly into a heavy slumber. What awoke him he could not say. An impression of the bedroom door closing hung in the air like an echo. The room was totally dark, all was quiet. King had the queerest feeling that someone was watching him. No, more than watching, studying him, waiting for some action on his part. He leaned over and pulled the switch on the lamp. It's dull yellow glow extended barely further than the centre of the room. All corners were in darkness, a darkness that was suggestively thick and tangible.

The feeling of being watched increased. It seemed to come from one particular corner of room. A faint odour assailed King's nostrils, as of old paper being burnt. He thought he could make out a darker shadow in the gloom, squat, man-shaped, featureless.

"Who's there? What do you want?"King stammered, icy fear slowly travelling up his spine. There came no reply except a dessicated, wordless rasp, the death rattle of something already dead.

From the corner of his eye, King noticed a movement, then another, then more! With a horrified start he saw, from all around, spiders, scores of them, of all shapes and sizes. From every part of the skirting, the floorboards, the ceiling they were coming, as though every spider in the old building had been summoned to his oasis of light. A deliberate crawling, creeping... across the floor and up onto the bed. Then a soft plop as one, then more, began falling onto the bedcovers from above.

With a slow, hideous inevitability, the wave of creatures amassed on the bed, onto and over the quivering form of King. He remained frozen in terror, locked rigid with revulsion, as the spiders ran hither and thither across his arms, legs and torso.

Not until a huge specimen ran across his face could King move. Voicing an inarticulate cry, he bounded for the door, rushed out of his room and stumbled down the stairs into the kitchen. It was there that Mrs Earnshaw found him when she came in early that morning, crouched under the table, a sobbing wreck. King never did return to that room.

Finding poor Mr King like that was a shock for Mrs Earnshaw. The poor young man was in a real funk. She gathered he had suffered some especially vivid nightmare - too much rich food no doubt! In any case, he borrowed a coat from one of the downstairs lodgers and went off to his sister's, asking for his belongings to be sent on later.

To be fair, when Mrs Earnshaw checked his room, there did seem to be a large number of spiders in the bed. Squashed, still and lifeless, but there nonetheless. No doubt there had been some hatching nearby; this was an old house after all. Poor Mr King had the misfortune to be present and this is what fermented his nightmare, she was sure.

But over the coming days Mrs Earnshaw noticed further oddities. She prided herself on keeping a clean house, but observed a considerable increase in cobwebs and dust around the place, most conspicuously up on the top floor. She couldn't understand it, she was always very particular with the cleaning. The missing cat? Well it wasn't unknown for cats to disappear for days at a time, though Missy never did return. There was that Mr Parker, too, he would no longer allow Mrs Earnshaw into his room to clean it. He left his washing out on the landing for her and she noticed the cobwebs on his clothing.

The oddest thing of all happened when she was up on the top floor one evening and heard Mr Parker in conversation. Not that she's the nosy type, of course, but she couldn't help overhearing. It sounded like an argument, Mr Parker pleading it seemed. There came a reply, but Mrs Earnshaw couldn't make out any clear words. The voice was "whispery and dry" she said, it reminded her of her brother, who came back from the war with gas damage.

In any case, she had to move back sharply as an agitated Parker burst out of the door and, after locking it behind him, stormed off down the stairs. Funny thing though, she got a good view into the room as he came out and there didn't appear to be anyone else in there.

◆

Lethbridge glances once more at the clock and continues.

"Parker was rarely seen out at that time - and when people did see him they remarked on his behaviour. He appeared nervous, in high dudgeon even. He cast frequent glances over his shoulder. His appearance, once so smart, had gone to seed, his clothes dusty, his hair wild. A number of people saw him on that last evening, hurrying through town. He was carrying what looked like a tool bag over one shoulder and a large satchel under one arm. He was seen furtively hanging around at the entrance to the old library building and that was the last anyone saw of him until.... well, until later"

◆

Parker stands at the top of the steps panting. He has no

eyes for the quiet early evening traffic or people moving about him on their business. His mind is fixed firmly on one goal.... to get rid of *him*. Glancing through the glass of the entrance door, he waits until the porter at the main desk moves up and away, called off on some errand or other. Parker immediately pushes through the doors and hurries up the staircase.

The first floor corridor is quiet and empty. Moving to the library door, he removes a crowbar from the tool bag over his shoulder. Applying it near the lock, he levers back and forth until, with a sharp crack, the door springs open. Parker glances around, then moves into the room, exchanging the crowbar for a torch. Turning it on, he takes the keys from the desk and walks swiftly to the other end of the room.

Unlocking the storeroom, he moves to the chest. Placing the torch on a shelf, Parker opens the chest and unwraps the iron box. He is about to unlock it, when the smell of burnt paper touches his nostrils. It is swiftly followed by sounds... a dry rustling, then a whispery rasp from desiccated lungs. A breath from something that doesn't need to breathe.

He stands, knocking the torch as does so. Its beam plays wildly around the room and onto the doorway. A hand appears round the frame, brown, withered, followed by that terrible, parchment-like face. Hairless with shallow, empty eye sockets, a stub of a nose and a lipless gash of a mouth. A thing of cobwebs and dust, a husk born of darkness and given life by some unholy process. A spider runs across the face as, with another airless sigh, the figure moves towards him, hands outstretched. Parker screams.

◆

Lethbridge stands up and stretches his back. "There is little more to tell. The porter was alerted by Parker rushing howling down the stairs, arms flailing, then crashing through the doors. Outside, he fell down the steps, picked himself up, then ran straight into the path of an oncoming brewer's lorry. It was not going particularly fast, but Parker went under the wheels and... well his death, at least, was instantaneous. Only one more thing remains to report. Those on the scene, including the doctor that attended, remarked that Parker had a thick layer of cobwebs across his face; "like a caul," the lorry driver described it. When the doctor removed it a host of small, pale spiders scurried off and away. He said he's never seen anything like it."

The shadows lengthen and Lethbridge clicks on the desk lamp. It enfolds the group in a circle of light, beyond which the bookcases stand like monoliths in the crepuscular gloom.

"Well, this is all well and good," says Beaumont, "but I can't fathom the relevance of half of this! Dollond told me about the damage to the door, it's been repaired. All the books here have been moved to the new site at West Road. Why on earth should we seal an empty room?"

"Not all the books have been removed Vice Chancellor," Lethbridge frowns. "The title in question remains, returned to the chest in the rear storeroom there. The iron box, however, has vanished without trace. It seems that whatever came out with the book has no desire to go back in again."

Dean Heywood harrumphs . "So you are telling us what Lethbridge, that this room is haunted? That some fiend lurks amongst the bookshelves?"

Lethbridge shrugs his shoulders and smiles sardonically. The room is completely dark now, excepting the lamp's circle of light. Two sounds float from the darkness; a dry rustle followed by a papery wheeze. All become aware of the smell of old, dusty paper. A pale-bodied spider suddenly scuttles into the circle of light, runs across the floor and disappears beneath the desk.

It might almost be seen as humorous, the sight of so many distinguished figures all fighting to get through a doorway at once. Even the unflappable Lethbridge, the thought of what might be behind him, cannot resist the urge to hurry as he flicks off the lamp and follows the group out, closing the heavy door with relief.

◆

And so it was that the old library room was sealed, locked tight, and has remained so ever since, by order of the Chancellor. Perhaps one day someone will open it - I wonder what they will find?

THE SCARECROW

The black and green scarecrow as everyone knows
Stood with a bird on his hat and straw everywhere.
He didn't care   – Syd Barrett

I couldn't tell you where or when I first saw the
scarecrow. It could have been five years ago or ten.
These days I find it hard to think or remember, I seem to sink
more and more into a vague haze. I do recall a long drive,
wide grey sky above the endless drove, straight and narrow
across fields of black earth. Pylons march like iron giants into
the distance. An old pillbox squats like a toad. Up a long track
a solitary farmhouse, dark windows staring at the road. And
there ahead, a figure in the field, face turned toward us. Is it
here to warn us or to scare away the crows? Only the farmer
knows.

As we get closer his features become clearer. The old
ragged coat, the oversize gloves, the hat, the smooth mask-
like face. As we get nearer he becomes more real, even
though we can see the post that keeps him fixed firmly in
place. Our car surfs by with barely a sound. Does his head
turn to watch as we pass, I wonder? Is it my imagination that
catches a movement in the mirror glass? And then he is gone,
just a speck in the wide, wide field as we head towards
another spot on the horizon.

But sometimes they surprise you. You might be walking
through the trees, perhaps to a picnic, soft summer breeze,
when suddenly he is there. From nowhere you feel his blank
stare as he waits at the corner of the field. You climb over the
gate and the person who is last wonders once again – does he
turn to watch as we wander past?

If I turn quickly will I see him move? A slight change of the arm perhaps? How could we ever prove it? I suppose these days you could set up a camera, film him all day. Do you think he would move if he knew we were watching? He is craftier than that. Beneath that old hat his eyes see everything.

But worst of all is seeing him where he is not supposed to be. That's the scariest part for me. Out of the corner of my eye, while in an old churchyard once I - but no, you will not believe. You will call me tired or emotional or perhaps under the influence of some deep seated need to be… different.

Nevertheless. A short cut, time saved. A path picked through the graves. Grey and austere, in contrast to the bright orange leaves in which they stand. A grey autumn day. And then – a hand? At the corner of the wall… no, not a hand, a glove! Crows caw and lift above. Did I wait to see the face? No… I ran …as fast as my feet could take me. Away from that place and back to the street, with cars and people and solid concrete beneath my feet.

Could he follow me there? I think not. There is safety in numbers. Not like in the Fen, where you are alone with them. A small pink dot upon the face of the dark, damp earth. Insignificant. What are we worth? Is that why they are here? To remind us, silently mocking? For when we are gone they still stand, watching and waiting.

I am safest in the house. Doors locked, curtains pulled, nothing gets in. But I have to go out. For food, you see, and that's when he has his chance. I know he is there; I catch a small glance every now and then. Just out of the corner of my eye. A glove… the blank face. Of course when I turn quickly there is no trace. Just a child's balloon or some old man in a coat, but I'm not fooled. I double my speed, get jobs done quick. Sometimes I'll take the bike, he can't keep up with that. The bell rings, sometimes I even sing as I ride it. There is a joy in that kind of freedom don't you think? I know people stare, what does it matter? As long as he is not there.

But today has been bad. It started this morning when I awoke at nine and looked out of the window. The house over the road has a tall hedge. And just over the edge of it I could see... the top of a hat. He must have followed me. How I don't know... but he knows where I live now. Where shall I go? No – stay here, lock all the doors, keep everything closed. Now that is all done I must stay perfectly still.. that way he will not know I am here.

But I have to be sure – there's a sound at the door! Rattle and clunk... ah, just the postman, delivering junk. I shall leave it there, he could see my silhouette through the glass. I shall stand here and wait. Just let the time pass.

The room grows dark. Long shadows fall on the wall. But I daren't turn on the light, he might see. Is he still there I wonder? How long can he wait ... shall I look.... a quick peek through the curtains....

Oh my God, he's there at the gate! Angles and thin, his eyeless face looking straight in! I gasp and retreat, pacing the room. What to do now? Stay or flee? Hide here in the gloom or take my chances outside?

The bike! Back garden shed! If I can make it to that I can be gone! Away like a swallow, a swift, a crow. He can't keep up he moves so slow... and yet... deliberate. With thick fingers I fumble at the back-door bolts. The door opens a crack and I peer out. Nothing. No-one. Just moonshine and the washing line. The paving stones to the shed shine like a stairway to salvation. Quietly, slowly, carefully I squeeze through the gap.

I close the back door behind me with a soft click, then pause, holding my breath.

The only sound is of distant passing traffic, like waves down on the beach. One step and then another along the path. At the shed door now, it opens with a creak! Will he hear? Is he near? I look round, there is nothing there. Carefully I lift out the bike. The chain! It has come loose, is this all in vain? No, think, think... now I kneel and put back on the chain, holding the bike by the frame.

A shadow falls across me. Something touches my hand... leathery and hard. A rough, old glove... and then above.....as I look up... his face... that mask bearing down... the eyes are so dark.... so dark.....

The farmer trudges slowly across the muddy field to the small bare rise of dark earth. A wooden pole lay on the ground. He crouches down to examine it then stands up, slowly turning round and round to look for any sign of his missing scarecrow.

"Bloody kids!" he mumbles to himself before taking the long walk back to the farmhouse.

Remnants

FENLAND GROUND IS SOFT FOR DIGGING

G eoff Newell smiled at his wife Betty as he carried the last book-filled box in through the front door "That's the lot love, I think we deserve a nice cuppa, don't you?"

All in all the move had gone well. The farm cottage was just the right size for the two of them. There was a spare bedroom he could use as an office and Pidley Fen was convenient for his work too, being halfway between the new sites at Peterborough and Head Office at Cambridge.

Geoff carried the boxes into the upstairs back room and placed them alongside his drawing board and rolls of plans. Living here meant he could largely work from home, driving up to Peterborough as needed, to supervise and liaise with the building companies.

The house itself was modest, not much more than a two up two down, set on the edge of the village. It was originally part of Church Lane Farm and overlooked the now empty and overgrown old farmhouse and yard. Other than that there was nothing but fields and fens as far as the eye could see. Geoff worried that Betty would get bored out here, but she had family within cycling distance at Warboys and assured him she would find plenty to do. "In any case," she reminded him, "you'll be under my feet most of the time, I expect I'll have plenty to do tidying up your mess!"

The whistling kettle brought him back to the present. He carried the mug upstairs and settled in at his new board, positioned close to the window for the best light. Turning to his left he looked out of the window and over at the old farmhouse, just the other side of the hedge. The place looked run down and gloomy. In the late afternoon light, the low sun flashed orange like flame in its windows. A movement caught his eye, a glimpse of something white in an upstairs window. But the place was empty, Geoff thought, it must have been the reflection of a passing bird. He turned back to his board and rolled out the plans for the new wing at Peterborough County Grammar School.

On those evenings when Betty was away at her sister's, Geoff took to strolling down to the village pub, The Mad Cat. The usual regulars were always in place, part of the furniture it seemed. Bernard, the local butcher, was the focal point, a large, florid man whose girth and complexion spoke of the dedicated drinker.

"Ah, here's our new boy!" boomed Bernard as Geoff entered the snug. "How's you finding our country ways lad, must be a shock for a city slicker?"

Bernard's companions laughed along. Geoff grinned, it was all good natured stuff and he wanted to be part of the community.

"Oh you know, Bernard old chap, getting used to it. Of course the lack of caviar and a butler is a constant strain!"

The assembled laughed and Bernard raised his glass in salute.

Soon Geoff was settled in with a pie and a pint, talking this and that with the locals. Almost all of them were farmers or farm workers it seemed.

"With so much farming round here, how come the farmhouse up by us is empty?" Geoff asked.

A silence settled over the company, many eyes in the group were downcast.

"Oh, you know, "said Bernard, "people move on, or sometimes they have no family to take over the place. Another round lads? Anyone fancy a game of darts?"

Geoff thought nothing more of the old farm until a few weeks later. He was working up in the back room one afternoon, when a creaking and banging sound from outside caught his attention. He put his head through the open window and saw that there was a door swinging open and closed on the outbuilding next to the farmhouse. Geoff put down his pen, went downstairs and out into the small cottage garden. The hedge was high and overgrown, so it was difficult to see anything from here. Geoff found a small gate in the corner of the garden and pushed it open.

The hinges squealed as Geoff stepped through into the old farmyard. Bits of equipment lay scattered about; weeds were growing through in most places. The farmhouse looked larger here, looming up over him. Nothing showed through the dark windows, they all seemed rather dirty, except for one upstairs window which looked like it had a circle cleared in the dirt.

Geoff walked over to the shed. The door was swinging to and fro, hinges loudly protesting. Geoff became aware of how silent the yard was. Apart from the door, there was no other sound... no birds, not even the rustle of a breeze. Slowly Geoff reached out a hand to open the door. His fingers closed on the old latch handle and he pulled the door towards him. A sudden burst of movement sent him reeling back, a flurry of black, a screech, Geoff fell back onto the ground.

The rook continued its flight, cawing loudly as it disappeared across the fields. Geoff let out a breath and got to his feet, wiping his hands and dusting himself down. He shut the door and walked back to the gate. His pulse took some time to settle and wasn't helped by the odd feeling he had of being watched. The house loomed over his shoulder,a brooding presence. Geoff wheeled.... was there a movement again? The upstairs window, a white blob, moving quickly away out of sight?

Geoff stood rooted to the spot in a haze of indecision. The farmhouse was empty, locked up in fact. He could see a heavy padlock on the front door. Should he go in and check? But how? Force the lock, break a window? It was probably just his imagination in any case; the bird had him spooked. His mind was made up by his wife's voice calling from the cottage garden

"Darling, I'm back, are you out here?"

He turned back to the cottage and made his way through the gate, resisting the temptation to look at the house again.

Geoff said nothing to his wife of the incident and it soon slipped to the back of his mind. Work got even busier and he was spending more and more time at the various sites in Peterborough. It only came back to mind when he arranged the meeting with Tom Harvey, senior partner at the practice. Rather than the house, Geoff arranged to meet Tom at The Mad Cat, much nicer to discuss work over a pint or two.

It was a cold January night when Geoff took a brisk walk down to the pub. The door opened into the agreeable fug of a log fire warmth, the haze of tobacco and the sound of general chat and laughter. Bernard was in place as usual, already a few pints ahead from the look of it.

"Ah our resident architect! How goes it young man, built any palaces yet?"

"Evening Bernard, evening lads, not yet, but when I do I'll make sure you get a wing to yourself," smiled Geoff

Glancing around, Geoff couldn't see Tom anywhere, so thought he might as well join the company. He placed his plans on a nearby table and ordered a pint. Standing to the side he listened to the conversation, mostly on farming matters and, in particular, the rising cost of land.

"That's one thing I don't understand," he interjected during a lull. "With the high demand for land, how come the old farm stands empty? I'd have thought it would have been snapped up by now."

"Not after what happened there," one of the locals muttered.

"Now, now," said Bernard, " no need to bring up all that old nonsense. Life's too short to be dwelling on the past and full of enough interesting things without having to speculate on tittle-tattle and gossip."

Geoff's interest was piqued. "What did happen there?" he asked. Several of the company turned away, mumbling about having to get home or "just nipping outside for a bit."

Bernard looked uncomfortable. "Well I supposed you'll hear about it sooner or later." He glanced meaningfully at his near empty glass. Geoff took the hint and ordered another pint. Satisfied by this, Bernard sighed, rubbed a hand over his face and began.

"Church Lane Farm had been owned by the Jakes family for generations. Frank was the last one to live there. He wasn't the easiest man to get along with. In fact he was a surly character, dangerous when he had a few drinks in him. He was eventually barred from this place after one punch up too many.

Anyhows he married this girl from up Warboys way, Anne Samuel was her name. Pretty girl but a bit of an odd one.

She moved in with him and all seemed to be going well, though she was never seen much in the village - and when she was people didn't really have much to do with her. Like I said, she was a bit odd and, of course, people round here have long memories - especially with the name Samuel. Then there were Frank's temper too, one time he came out after her, screaming and shouting in the street, accusing her of this and that. Apparently he'd heard that she'd been chatting to a lad down by the churchyard.

No-one really saw much of her at all after that, even those who visited the farm. I delivered there now and then. I used to see her looking out of the window at me. Some wondered if old Frank had locked her up.

That was that, then we heard as how an aunt of Anne's had passed on and left her some big old place up at Warboys. That, no doubt, would have been worth a bob or two. Still, no-one saw her much and then, after a while, no-one saw her at all. Frank still came into the village, but no-one dared ask him. No-one except me that is. I don't like bullies, never have. He was in the shop one day, so I asked him straight.

"She's gone," he said, "left me, gone off, who knows where?"

"Have you spoken to her family? Is she alright?" I asked.

Well old Frank goes right off at me.

"What's it to do with you? You mind your own affairs! Don't you go sticking your nose in, shut up or I'll...."

Frank had puffed himself up, raised his fists even, but he then noticed the large cleaver I'd been chopping the meat with. So he turns and storms out the shop, slamming the door. Well you can imagine the gossip that caused and, in due course, someone notified the local police.

I hear tell how they went up to the farm and Frank wouldn't let them in. So they went back with a warrant and searched the around for a bit."

"Well, what did they find?" I asked.

"Nothing, "Bernard continued. "They looked round the house, her clothes had gone, there was no sign of her. But when they checked, her family hadn't seen her either. So that was it."

"That was it? There was no investigation, he wasn't charged?"

"There was no evidence see, nothing at all and you have to remember our police out here aren't like your city lot. They don't have much to work with and, to be honest, they like a quiet life. She was filed as missing and that was that. Of course, us in the village had our own ideas."

"What do you mean?" I asked.

"Well.... we have a saying out these parts. Fenland ground is soft for digging." Bernard took a long draft from his beer and fell silent.

"Course, that weren't the last of it. It was about a year ago, some months after the police had been in. It was the people who lived in the cottage before you, Old Bob and his wife Mary. They were woken up one night by a man screaming. Coming from the farmhouse, it were. So they goes out, but can't see anything. Then the screams stop. Old Bob tells me he went back in to get a torch, then made his way over to the farm. He told me he thought he saw someone at the window as he walked back, but when he got into the house.... well there was only one person in there. Frank Jakes, laid out in his bed. Stone dead he was. Bob told me his face was torn to pieces, like an animal had clawed him. Yet his eyes were still there, wide open, Bob said, bulging, like he was terrified.

Well, the police were back in of course. There was no sign of an intruder, so, despite the wounds, the official verdict was 'heart attack'. They put the wounds down to a farm cat. No one was in much of a mind to investigate any further, to be honest. Bob and his wife moved out not long after, to his daughter's at Norwich. Frank had no living kin, so the old farm has been empty ever since. None of the locals wanted anything to do with it."

I was about to ask another question when a hand suddenly gripped my shoulder.

"Geoffrey old son, how are you?" It was Tom. "Sorry I'm late, the bloody car wouldn't start. New Rover 60, wouldn't mind but I've only had it a few weeks! Anyway, I'll have a G and T, then we can get started!"

All thoughts of the farm fled Geoff's mind and the rest of the evening was spent in going over plans for one of the new developments. A productive meeting and a few more drinks later, Tom dropped Geoff off back home. Betty was already in bed reading.

Before joining her, Geoff went into his office to put his papers away. He glanced over at the old farmhouse. Silent and dark it stood, the thin moonlight reflected in the top floor windows. Geoff felt a growing sense of unease, which he put down to Bernard's lurid stories and those last two brandies. He turned away and went to bed.

Geoff came awake with a start. The echoes of a man's scream rang in his ears.... was it real or had he dreamt it? Betty lay breathing softly beside him, deep in sleep. The alarm clock said 3.35.

Geoff sighed and got up, putting on his dressing gown and slippers. Going across the hall to the bathroom, he happened to glance into the office. Through the window opposite he caught a glimpse of the farmhouse. There.... what was that? He moved into the office. There it was again, definitely a movement in the upstairs window.

Could it be a burglar? Maybe some itinerant had broken into the place? Geoff strode down the stairs. A quick delve in the scullery produced a large, old torch and a chisel. Taking both, he slipped quietly out of the cottage, across the garden and through the gate.

The yard and house were totally silent. The new moon cast very little light, but with a couple of taps Geoff got the torch to work. Moving round to the rear of the farmhouse, Geoff found the back door secured with a small hasp and padlock. Determined to get to the bottom of things, he set thechisel in place and with a couple of sharp yanks pulled the hasp free. Geoff slowly opened the door and stepped over the threshold.

The first thing that struck him was the smell. Musty, stale, old cooking, tobacco. He stepped into a sparsely furnished kitchen. Shining the torch around, he searched in vain for a light switch. There was none, in fact there was no fitting or bulb. It seemed electricity had not reached here yet.

The torch began to flicker. Geoff tapped it a couple of times and the beam of light steadied. He moved into the hallway. The living room stood off to one side, the front door was ahead and a staircase led up into the gloom. The floor was piled high with stacks of old newspapers and what looked like bills and letters. The musty smell grew stronger.

Geoff played the torch up towards the front door. A man's cap hung on a hook, a stout walking stick leaned against the wall. On a small table stood an old oil lamp. The torch flickered again. Geoff picked up the lamp - it had some oil in it still. Reaching into his dressing gown pocket, he took out his pipe and matches. Placing the torch on the table, he lit the oil lamp. The warm glow spread around the hall, though did nothing to make the place feel cosier.

Carrying the lamp and the torch, Geoff moved back towards the kitchen. At that moment a sound from upstairs froze him to the spot. A scraping sound, short and sharp... perhaps of a chair being moved or a door opened. Geoff moved to the foot of the stairs. Placing the lamp on the floor he began to ascend, playing the torch beam out ahead of him.

The torch revealed an old, worn carpet and poorly painted walls. The stairs creaked under Geoff's slow tread. He came to a dark landing, the stairs turning up and to the left. Geoff continued, one hand clutching the banisters for support.

Two things happened. The torch went out... and Geoff felt a hand on his hand. It was ice cold... thin, wiry... but with a firm grip. He could feel sharp nails digging into his skin....

With a gasp Geoff desperately hit the torch against his leg several times. The beam came back on and shone directly up into a face barely a foot away from Geoff's own. Waxen, white skin stretched tightly over the bony features. Lank, black hair framed the face, the darkened lips were pulled back over yellowed teeth, the eyes bulged with a mad, hateful fire.

But that wasn't the worst thing. With rising horror, Geoff saw that one side of the head was missing, caved in! With revulsion he realised he could see inside... and there were things in there.... wriggling things!

With a scream, Geoff wrenched his hand free and flung his hands up as if to block out the awful sight. In so doing, he fell backwards, hitting the wall behind him then crashing down the stairs. There was a burst of orange, then darkness and Geoff fell into blessed oblivion.

A murmur of voices.... a sense of movement.... Betty's face fading in and out... darkness once more. Then something moving... Betty? No, it was that terrible face again and a scream, an agonised man's scream!

Geoff awoke with a start. Sitting up, he immediately felt faint, groaned and sank back down again.

"Easy there lad," it was Bernard's voice, "take it easy now, you've had a nasty bump."

"Where am I?" Geoff struggled to focus in his surroundings.

"You're in hospital boy. You been in the wars. But nothing more than a concussion and a sprained wrist it seems."

"But the house.... what... how did I get here?"

"Well you can thank your wife for that - she saved you! She says she heard you going out of the cottage, then through the garden gate. So she got up and followed you. Lucky for you she did. She found you at the bottom of the stairs in the old place, out for the count. A lamp had gone over and there was a tidy little fire going. She dragged you out, then ran down to the phone box for an ambulance and fire brigade."

"Oh my God... the woman.... did she see the woman?" Geoff became agitated.

"Now then, calm down boy. There was no-one else there, she said. And if there was, well.... the place has burned to the ground. The fire caught hold, by the time the fire brigade arrived from Ramsey the place was a mass of flames. Good riddance, some might say!"

"I must get back, Betty, is she... how long have I been here?"

"Betty's fine.... and you've been out for two days. She has been sat here for all of that, I just came in a short while ago to give her a break. She'll be back presently. The police were in earlier too, they may want to speak to you later."

"I thought they'd lost interest in the place?"

"Ah this was some important type out of Cambridge. Seems that boss of your has friends in high places! There was a

Detective of some sorts and a couple of foot soldiers out yesterday looking over the place. Funny thing they found, the Detective was telling me."

"Was it....was it a body?" asked Geoff.

"No," Bernard leant in, stroking his chin, "it was a hole in the ground. A large hole, tucked well away behind some old machinery at the back of the yard. About six feet deep they said, a pit, with all the earth chucked out at the sides. And in the pit they found two things... a crowbar clotted with dried blood and hair, and a woman's shoe."

"But apart from that it was empty?" Geoff grasped Bernard's arm with his good hand. "How could that be?"

"Well it's like I said boy. Fenland ground is soft for digging... and that's digging in or digging out...."

Remnants

MISSION THIRTEEN

"**S**teady, keep it steady Skip......bombs gone! Bombs gone!" Prepared as he was for the sudden lift as the Lancaster discharged its heavy load, Johnson still struggled to keep the bomber straight.

As it was the sudden rise brought them smack into a searchlight cone. Dazzling, white light filled the cockpit as one beam, then another, transfixed the bomber. The unwelcome light was quickly followed by flak. Johnson twisted and turned the bomber. The RAAF Lanc was surprisingly manoeuvrable for such a large plane, but the gunners of Cologne were on form tonight. The aircraft shuddered as a huge bang exploded close to port.

"Sod this for a laugh!" muttered Flight Engineer Barnes from his seat in the cockpit.

Johnson addressed the crew. "Hold on chaps, this is going to be interesting!"

Under his strong hands the bomber twisted into a corkscrew climb, before diving off to starboard and turning for home. Darkness reigned again apart from the glow of the instruments and the distant glow from Cologne.

"Report in," said Johnson

"OK here Skip." said Barnes

"Venning, all clear up front!" from the front turret

"Farmer, ok! " came the navigators voice

"Lynch, all ok here skip!" called the radio operator

"Gibbo, all present and correct!" from the mid-gunner.

" You trying to wake me up from my nap, Skip?" Chuckled Prestworth, the tail gunner.

"Alright lads, settle in, let's get back home."

Other Lancs were already forming for the return flight. Johnson set course to get back into some kind of formation, there was safety in numbers.

"Port engine two is coughing a bit skip." noted Barnes

"Alright, keep an eye on it, let me know if-"

"Bandit! Bandit! Port aft!" Gibson's voice screamed over the tannoy, followed by the chatter of his twin machine guns.

His own guns were echoed by cannon shells ripping through the port side of the Lanc. Sparks flew as the bomber reeled from the impact, cordite and smoke filled the forward fuselage.

Johnson immediately put the plane into a steep dive, once again twisting and turning, like a hare from the hounds.

"Gunners, what have we got?"

"No sign here, Skip," from Venning

"Nothing here either, Skip," came Gibson's reply

"Same here," from the tail gunner, "looks like we lost him."

"Skip.... we've both been hit," came Farmer's voice, "Lynch is in a bad way."

Johnson turned to Barnes "Take a dekko back there Tom, see what's what."

In the meantime he brought the plane down to four thousand feet and resumed homeward course. There was no sign now of either their attacker, or the rest of the squadron.

Barnes returned. "Not good skip, he shook his head, "Farmer has cuts and scratches, but Lynch got a direct hit, shoulder, he's losing blood fast. The radio is rooted, smashed to pieces. Farmer managed to put the fire out, but the equipment looks done for."

"OK Tom. Get Lynch as comfortable as you can, I'll get us back as quick as possible. Nothing else can go wrong surely!"

It was at that moment that number three engine began to splutter, cough and finally die out.

"Bloody hell!" Johnson swore, "mission thirteen is living up to expectation!"

The thought took him back to that afternoon's briefing back at Binbrook...

◆

"Mission thirteen, eh Johnno?" Squadron Leader MacDonald nudged Johnson with a grin and for good measure prodded him with his pipe.

"Yes Chief. I'm not the superstitious kind, but this one has me spooked for some reason."

"Don't you worry Johnno, you've got a good crew and in any case I'll be out there too, I'll see you right. Now, let's see what the bods have in store for us shall we?"

MacDonald led the way into the briefing room, where the rest of the crews were already assembled. Low chat and cigarette smoke filled the room. The CO entered with two officers and there was an expectant hush.

"Alright chaps, settle down!" announced the CO.

"Our Spy here, Benton, will be giving you all the details of tonight's little jaunt. I know he's a Pom, but do pay attention now, we don't want anyone losing their way this time... do we Thommo?"

The crews laughed with good humour at the reddening Thompson whose last mission somehow ended on the Isle of Wight.

"Thank you sir," Benton stepped up and revealed the large wall map. "OK chaps, its Cologne......"

The briefing over, the crewmen began filing out of the room. Benton was gathering his papers back into his folder. "There you go Johnno" said MacDonald, "piece of cake, eh?

Just stick with me, I'll get you back in one piece."

"No worries Chief," Johnson smiled, "it's just a number right?"

Then Johnson noticed Benton staring intently at the Squadron Leader, his face pale. "You ok sir", he asked.

"What, oh, yes.... er fine, yes, sorry. Well.. .good luck chaps!" Benton placed his folder under his arm and headed out of the room.

◆

"Skip.....Skip...." Barnes voice brought Johnson back to the here and now.

"Yes Tom what is it?"

"Sorry Skip.....Lynch is gone."

Johnson closed his eyes and muttered an oath.

"OK, thanks Tom."

He took a minute to compose himself then addressed the whole crew.

"Alright chaps I won't sweeten it. Lynch has bought it, Farmer's wounded. We are one engine down and have no radio. Navigation is somewhat buggered up but I'll do my best to bring us in over the East Coast. Once there we can hopefully pick up a light or signal and we'll be having tea in the mess in no time. Keep watching, gunners, let's hope there no more of those fighter bastards out there. Chin up chaps, we're due a bit of good luck"

Limping on its three engines the battered Lancaster made slow progress across the cold, dark North Sea. The drone of the engines, the aftermath of the adrenaline rush and the endless darkness around them conspired to make them all drowsy, each man sunk deep in his own thoughts.

"Hot soup, Skip?"

Barnes nudged Johnson, with a start he turned, accepting the thermos.

"Thanks Tom. Damn.... look at this!" Johnson indicated the fuel gauge, "we must be leaking it somewhere.... there's about an hour left, let's hope we hit the coast soon."

Johnson began a shallow descent to bring them over the coast. As he did so the plane became enveloped in thick fog

"Hells teeth, will nothing go right tonight!"

Effectively, the plane was blind. There were no lights below, black out was still in force. In any case the thick fog brought vision down to a minimum.

"There's no choice Tom," Johnson" grimaced, "get the lads ready to bail out. Once you're gone I'll turn back over the coast and jump. The crate can ditch in the sea, I'm not having it go down over land, it could hit anything."

"OK Skip. I'll stay here if it's all the same, you'll need a hand. Besides, the fish-heads will pick us up," replied Bates with a grin.

Both men knew it was as good as a death sentence. Unless they were found very quickly they would freeze to death in the February North Sea.

"Alright, let's tell the lads."

"Skip, Skip! There's something coming alongside us, it's signalling." Gibson's voice burst over the intercom. "It's a Lanc, Skip, it's one of ours!"

Both men turned to look out of the glass canopy. Sure enough the shape of a Lancaster loomed out of the mist, slightly below and to starboard. He had all his nav lights on and was flashing a call sign.

"C for Charlie - stone me it's the Squadron Leader!" said Barnes.

"Ha ha the old bugger, he said he'd see us home!" laughed

Johnson.

The other Lanc moved into position forward of them and they followed it in. Soon they began a landing descent and the lights of the airfield became visible below. Johnson nursed the heavy plane down, the wheels hit tarmac, bounced, then hit again and screeched.

Within minutes the plane was taxiing to the end of the runway, support vehicles already racing towards them. Johnson made his way down the steps, legs shaky as he reached terra firma once more. The rest of the crew gathered round, grinning in relief.

"Nice one Skip, you got us back!" said Gibson.

"Not me Gibbo, we've the Chief to thank for that one!"

He collared one of the passing ground crew.

"Hey mate, do you know where the Chief is? We owe him a drink or two!"

The erk seemed confused.

"Squadron Leader MacDonald, sir? Why, I suppose you haven't heard. A few of the other crews saw it. It was a direct hit from flak. The plane broke up immediately... the Chief went down over the target."

Remnants

THE SQUIRE

What's that? You'd like me to tell you a ghost story? OK.... well, where to begin? I could tell you about the old lady who used to come and tuck me in when I were a little boy. That was when we lived in the big old Victorian place in Barnsley, it's not there anymore, they knocked it down to build the new flyover.

In any case, I remember every night she used to come and look at me. I never felt scared, she had a very kind face, you see. I can still see her face clearly. I don't remember when she stopped coming, maybe I just grew up and didn't need tucking in anymore.

That was a strange old house. Do you know a few years ago I spoke to the people who moved in there after us? Yep, it was through Facebook, there was a picture of the old place on some group and we got talking. Turned out they had some strange things happen there too, like a dark figure looking in through the back garden window. My mum had seen the same thing too, years before. Funny how these things happen, eh?

Did anything else happen as I was growing up? No, not really. We moved to a new house in Manchester with Dad's new job, that place were fine. Course there was the usual stuff kids get up too. I remember a group of us going into the local boneyard one night. A goat popped its head up, scared the life out of us, Johnny Birkinshaw actually wet himself! The goat lived there see, they used it to keep the grass down.

My wife? Yes, well, that's when a lot of things changed. See, things always happened around her, even as a child. So for her it were nothing unusual - and it's not like stuff started happening straight away. First place we lived in together was fine, though she had her "little flashes" as she calls them, now and then. There was one strange Christmas - we'd been on a tour around Ordshall Hall. I'm convinced something latched onto her and followed us back home. For several weeks after we had strange things going on, drawers opening, banging on the cupboard door. We called it Peter the Poltergeist. I have some pictures somewhere, you can see this weird streak of light on them. Not sure where they are - I don't know what happened to all my photos.

Anyway, that died down after a while. Then we moved down south to the Fens. It was her mother's house, you see, she had passed away and as Sarah was the only child she inherited the place. It fitted our plans, she'd just got the new job at with the trainer at Newmarket, so the place was ideally situated. Sure it were a big change, Manchester to the Fens, but you know, new start and all that.

Haunted? No, I don't think so. I mean, it was a bit of a creepy old place, right out in the sticks. But no, not haunted. Once it was cleaned up and redecorated it was very nice. I was able to work from home, we had the horses and the cats and dogs, it were all very pleasant. No, the haunted place was Lauren's house.

Lauren? Ah yes, she was a friend of Sarah's from way back. She was a lecturer, film and media studies I think, at NUA. To be honest I never really took to her, very much the hippy type and a bit of an old soak. Mind you, living in that place, it's no wonder I suppose. No, I mean her house, though the village itself is quite isolated - our place was rural but we weren't that far from town. Marshland St James is really way out in the Fens - the name tells you that, right?

We were in the new place a couple of weeks when Lauren

asked us up for lunch. It were only about a forty minute drive I suppose, as long as you don't get lost! You know what it's like out that way, long, straight roads, everywhere looks the same. Still, it was a nice sunny day, lovely wide blue sky, we had the top down on the MG. We found the Marsh Road turn-off and that led us further out into the Fens, nothing but fields and dykes as far as the eye could see. Eventually we came into the village itself.

It's like most places these days, I suppose, a quaint old village, a big church and manor house, then a modern estate whacked on the side, like a pimple on a pretty cheek. Lauren's place was near the church, close to the centre of the village. It was a detached house, three storied, with those typical, large Georgian windows and a dark, slate roof. Double fronted, with twin gables each side of the central front door, which was protected by a nice carved porch. Ivy covered a lot of the dark stone walls and the hedges at the front of the property were a bit overgrown. To be honest the whole place looked a bit shabby - but that 's Lauren I guess, shabby chic is her thing.

We pulled into the yard at the side of the house; there was a stable with a small paddock to the back and a large shed. As we got out of the car, a large black lab came out to greet us - all waggy tail and dribbles - closely followed by Lauren, wine glass in hand. She showed us through, down a couple of steps and into the kitchen. It was a large, country type kitchen, with a large old table in the centre of the room, a cat in the dog bed and the inevitable Aga. There were a couple of small windows high up in the walls. Lauren explained this was the oldest part of the house, thought to go back to mediaeval age. Most of the rest of the house had been renovated in Georgian times.

Inside was dark and cool after the bright sunshine and the

wine was poured, so things were fine. The two of them got chatting and I was left to my own devices. I went outside to give the horses a carrot each and the dog followed me. A strange thing happened then. This feller came walking past, I presumed he were a local. Despite the weather he was wearing this long overcoat, with the collar turned up, like some pensioners do in the summer I suppose, have you noticed that? Anyway, the dog starts going mad, barking, and growling. It ran up to the gate, it really had its hackles up, teeth bared. I've never seen a Labrador do that - I mean you expect that of a guard dog, like an Alsatian or Doberman perhaps, but not a daft old lab. Anyway the old boy looks over and hurries on past. Soon as he had gone, the lab was back to normal. Came waggling over to me again, panting.

By then the girls came out, Lauren said she was taking us up to the local pub for lunch. That was another experience! Oh, the food and all that was fine, it was the landlord. I made the mistake of asking for a lager top, you should have seen his face! You'd have thought I'd asked for some exotic cocktail. He sneered and virtually threw it at me. Charmed I'm sure, I thought. Anyway, we had lunch, walked back to the house, then drove back home, that was it.

Sarah went up to Lauren's a couple of times after that, though I managed to swerve off, on account of work or some other excuse. Lauren came down to us once or twice too, she usually ended up passed out drunk and we'd put her in the spare room. No, it were the second time I went up to her house that I had the bad experience. We were going for dinner this time; the plan was to stay over, then drive up to some other friends of ours in Lincoln the next day. We went into the kitchen same as last time and this time I got to see the rest of the ground floor. From the kitchen a couple of steps led up to a door which led onto a corridor running the length of the house. A staircase led up from this, then the corridor opened into a small hallway, dimly lit by the light through the glass of the front door. There was a downstairs loo and what used to be called a parlour at the front. At the end of the corridor were a large sitting room with a couple of couches and a TV. A glass door led out to a small courtyard garden at the side of the house. It was all bare wooden floors, dark wood and dark red walls, a bit oppressive and dark to be honest. It was in this room we settled, with a drink of course, while Lauren prepared dinner.

We ate the meal at the kitchen table, watched closely by old Reg the lab naturally! I say meal - it was a kind of pasta bake in some sauce. But there was very nice fresh bread and plenty of wine of course. Eventually Lauren did her passing out at the table trick again. I asked Sarah if we should move her, but she said no, this is where Lauren normally slept. So I let the dog out for a wee and brought our bags in from the car.

There were two bedrooms and a bathroom on the first floor, then, from what I gather another two small rooms up in the eaves. I took our bag up to the room were staying in. It were right by the stairs, there was a narrow corridor with the other bedroom door just opposite. I did notice something odd at the time - the other bedroom had a big old bolt on the outside of the door.

The room itself was quite large, with a large old fashioned double bed with its head set against the interior wall. The front window looked out onto the quiet village street. I unpacked a few things then went back down the stairs to get a glass of water. Old Reg sat at the foot of the stairs looking up at me. I beckoned him up towards me but he wouldn't move, he just whimpered. So I grabbed the cat instead, a lovely specimen, a big Maine Coon farm cat. I carried her up to the room and plonked her on the bed. To my surprise she hissed and ran straight out, back down the stairs. First time I've ever seen a cat turn down the chance to sleep on a bed! We turned in and, after all that wine, were both soon sound asleep.

I can't tell you what time it was I woke up, but I can tell you what I saw. I was on the right hand side of the bed. I looked over and in the gloom could make out a figure crouched over Sarah! Without thinking I threw a punch at it - complete reflex action, don't know why. It looked threatening I guess. Well the punch didn't connect with anything, but the figure straightened. It was totally black, like a silhouette. I couldn't make out any features but it was the shape of a man wearing a large coat and hat, like one of those old highwaymen or something.

Then the figure kind of faded... it moved slowly backward and blended into the darkness of the wall. There was no sound, total silence.... except for the pounding of my heart. The hairs on my arms were standing up on end. Sarah was still sound asleep. Even when I spoke to her and nudged her she didn't wake up.

I turned the light on and got up. There was nothing or no-one else in the room. The wall was solid. I was in a state of near panic; I never felt so scared in my life, every part of me was awake and aware. I got back into bed, but there was no way I was turning the light off. For a while everything was still.

Then I heard it. At first I thought it was my heart... but no, it was a banging.... someone or something was banging on the wall behind me at the head of the bed. I know that was impossible because the wall on the other side was the stairwell, no-one could reach unless they were on a step ladder or something. Bang, bang, bang... I covered my ears and tried to ignore it... bang... bang... bang. I don't know if the banging stopped before or after I fell asleep, but the next thing I remember was waking up and it was daylight. Sarah was already up and in the kitchen. I put on my dressing gown and went downstairs, there was a cooked breakfast on the go. I had two mouthfuls then had to rush to the loo to throw up. It was put down to a hangover and I didn't say anything about what happened until we were in the car and halfway up the A17.

Now the good thing about Sarah was you could talk about stuff like this with her. Let's face it, most people would laugh it off as a nightmare or too much wine. But she'd seen enough to know better. She was quiet while I related my tale and for a few minutes after. She then told me she had seen the same figure too - once before when she had stayed at the house overnight, in the other upstairs bedroom. She had been woken up by what she described as the mattress "curling around her," almost as though the bed was trying to wrap her up. The dark man was in the corner of the room. She told me she shouted at him to go away and fought against the bedclothes. He faded away. That's why we stayed in the other bedroom this time, she explained. But it seemed this figure was not confined to the one room.

She had done a bit of research round the village and asked Lauren a few questions. Lauren didn't say, much, but she did reveal she never slept upstairs. Most of the information came from the old geezer in the pub - bit of a stereotype eh?

Anyway, according to this guy, the house was once owned

by the local Squire, the main landowner in the area. In those days a guy like that was like God to the locals, they depended on him for work and housing. Turns out this guy were a baddun, liked to take his pick of the local girls. Any that took his fancy were taken on as maids at the house and.... well I'm sure you can imagine. Hence the bolt on the door, I suppose. The house had stayed in his family for a couple of generations, until the last old lady owner died and Lauren moved in.

How did that make me feel? Well, glad on the one hand that I hadn't had some weird hallucination - and a bit annoyed on the other hand that she hadn't said anything about it! How annoyed? Well, a bit I suppose, I weren't that mithered, just think she should have mentioned it .

Why did we go back to the house? It were a few months later, Sarah got a call from Lauren, she was ill, could we pop up, help with the horses, blah blah blah. I wasn't happy about going, but I wasn't going to let Sarah go on her own. So we found ourselves driving across the lonely Fens again. It weren't so pleasant this time; it was cold, grey sky, very gloomy. Maybe it was my imagination, but I thought the house looked darker and more rundown than before. Certainly the hedge still hadn't been trimmed.

Anyway, Lauren was in place at the table, the Aga was blasting out heat, Sarah and I fussed around sorting out the horses and the cat and dog. Then of course, she asked if we would mind staying over. You know, she said she had a bad cold, but I don't think Lauren was ill. She looked more scared to me - not nervous or twitchy but almost like a PTSD victim. Very quiet, withdrawn, like she wasn't there. Even the dog was quiet, he lay on his bed in the corner of the kitchen, head on paws.

Well what could we say? I looked at Sarah, she looked at me…. that was that, we were staying. Lauren bedded down on the couch and we headed up to the main bedroom again. So this time I thought well at least I can keep the light on all night. I'd be ready if anything happened. I could stay awake all night and keep an eye on things. That was the plan. Of course I nodded off.

I awoke with start. The light was off, only a pale moon glow lit the room. My breath was a steamy cloud. I sat up straight. At the foot of the bed a dark figure was…. materialising is the only way I can describe it. I tried to move but the sheets seemed tight about me. To my horror the bed… writhed. I felt the mattress shift under me, the sheets began winding themselves around me. I tried to shout but all that came out was a hoarse whisper. I turned to Sarah, I'll never forget the look on her face as long as I live. Her eyes were wide and shining in the moonlight, her face a mask of pure panic. Our struggles became stronger, yet the more we struggled the tighter the sheets became, covering our faces now, writhing, twisting, restricting. I heard Sarah scream, loud and piercing…. there was the sound of a dog howling… a banging on the door …. then darkness….

I'm sure you know the rest. Seems Lauren was woken by the scream, came up and found us, called an ambulance, called the police. I came around crouched in the corner of the room. They said I was babbling, incoherent. Sarah was dead… my Sarah… the sheet wrapped around her neck.

Well that's what happened. He got to her in the end, I couldn't do anything to save her. I don't know why he targeted my Sarah, perhaps he reminded her of someone, perhaps it was just because she was there. Perhaps because she fought him off before.... he came back stronger somehow.

What? You have to go now? Oh that's ok, I expect the nurse will be in with my medication soon. Will you visit and talk again? No? That's a shame, I've enjoyed speaking to you. Oh I see, you have enough for your report. Well thank you for talking to me and listening to my story - you see, most people don't believe me when I tell them it was the Squire that murdered Sarah.

Remnants

THE CONFESSION OF BROTHER SIMON

Tower Bruer Templar Preceptory, 29th October 1216

Abbot Thomas nodded to the gatekeeper as he was let into the courtyard and made his way into the preceptory. The journey from Kirkstead had been somewhat hurried and uncomfortable, but Abbot William's message had urged all possible haste, as well as discretion.

All Thomas knew was that he was to perform absolution for a person here at Tower Bruer. Once inside, he was led quickly into a side room and given some plain, but welcome, victuals. The room was small, lit by a few candles, furnished only with a table and two chairs. After a short time a young man came in to clear away the plate and cutlery. Almost as soon as he had left, a tall figure, dressed in monk's robes, entered and sat. Thomas could see little of the person's face, save something of the chin. The head remained bowed, hands held together within the long sleeves.

"Father forgive me, for I have sinned. I would make my confession," came a whispering but steady voice from the cowl.

"But of course Brother. Where would you like to begin?" The Abbot leaned forward attentively.

"By first saying, Abbot, that I am no Brother. I am not a monk, I am a Templar Knight. Forgive the deception, but it proved necessary for my task."

"And this task, the reason for this deception, it was some thing of great import my son?"

"Indeed it was Father - it was in order to murder King John!"

Croyland Abbey, 8th October 1216

As he nudged the pony across the narrow bridge and into the marketplace, Abbot William noticed at once the two burley, cowled figures ahead who moved towards him. While outwardly dressed as monks, it was clear they bore weapons and armour beneath the plain robes.

"Abbot William? I'm... Brother Simon," the lead figure took the pony's reins, while the other glanced about. "I've been asked to meet you and take you into the abbey."

"Very well... Brother, please lead on." William nodded and allowed himself to be led through the small market and into the grounds of the abbey. Dismounting and handing his horse to a young monk, William followed the two figures through an archway and along a short corridor, which ended in a stout wooden door. Brother Simon knocked sharply and the door opened a fraction. After a short pause it opened fully and William was ushered into the room, followed by Brother Simon. The other "monk" took up position outside the door.

"Ah Abbot William, such a pleasure to see you again!" A grey haired, elderly monk rose to greet William, black robes contrasting with his own white. He advanced, grasping William's hands. Elderly perhaps, but the grip and twinkle in the eye showed no sign of age or infirmity.

"Abbot Geoffrey," William smiled, "I see the years have been kind to you! Why the last time we met must have been in Cyprus, do you reme-"

"Harrumph!" coughed a corpulent figure seated at the room's large table "Much as I enjoy hearing old tales of derring-do I might remind you that we are here for important issues - and that this meeting is extremely hazardous to all!"

"Apologies Milord, you must forgive an old soldier. Allow

me to introduce Abbot William of Swineshead Abbey."
William stepped forward and bowed his head. Abbot Geoffrey
gestured to each in turn, beginning with the corpulent
nobleman.

"Robert de Gresely, Baron of Manchester. Abbot Adam of
Croxton, " this to a tall, thin monk. "Sir Simon of the Templar
order," this to the cowled figure who had brought William
here. "Hugh Bigod," a fresh faced young man half rose and
bowed. "and his father, Sir Roger Bigod."

A lean figure dressed in fine hose leant against the narrow
window ledge at the far end of the room. He turned and
bowed slightly to William, then stepped forward to the head
of the table to address the conspirators.

"Let us begin, gentlemen. Firstly, I'm sure I need not remind
you that no word of what passes here today shall leave this
room. Many of us have suffered already at the King's hand.
We wish to put an end to such suffering and tyranny. I'm sure
we all have our own reasons for wishing the King be.... gone"

"I'll say," huffed de Gresely, "he's already threatened to
increase the price of bread forty fold in order to fill his tax
coffers! Outrageous!"

"Indeed," agreed Abbot Geoffrey, "and let us not forget what
he has already done. Both Peterborough and our own Abbey
here were cruelly sacked by the tyrant, even the sacred
vessels were carried off! "

"The Guthlac Roll?" interjected Abbot Adam.

"We were fortunate to save that, by the grace of God,"
replied Geoffrey, "the looters were more inclined to earthly
rather than spiritual treasures."

"Many local estates have suffered similar" spoke the young
Hugh, "raids, punitive measures, taxation... it really is beyond
the pale!"

"I understand the King is not even beyond base blackmail concerning more.... delicate matters?" Geoffrey inclined his head towards the reddening Adam, who busied himself with the large bag at his feet.

"In any case," continued Sir Roger, "Dauphin Louis has landed in Kent and is moving towards London. King Alexander once again moves south from Scotland. If we make our play correctly, we will have the support of much of the nobility. However, if the King is obviously murdered then who knows how people will react? We not know where Marshall will stand, or any of those others who currently waver. Father Adam, you have some thoughts on this?"

Adam brought forth a collection of vials and jars from his bag.

"I have some experience with herbal matters. Here are a range of substances which will, if ingested, bring about death. There are two difficulties, though. The first is in administering the poison to the King. Each of these has a strong taste, which would be difficult to mask - and let us not forget the King is never without his taster! The second is that the effects of these herbs are widely known. It would be obvious to even a half-trained eye that the King has been poisoned. We can only wonder what repercussions that might bring on those present at the time."

"Why not more direct means?" the young Hugh stood, grasping the hilt of his dagger. "Get in close and finish it!"

"You forget the King's bodyguard," proffered Simon, "an armed person would not get within ten feet of the King, especially given his current state of mind. And if they did succeed they would be immediately cut down!"

"A person in disguise may be able to get close." Geoffrey arched his eyebrows, motioning to Simon's robes.

"True, but it is still a certain death mission, we could not expect anyone to do that, however just the cause," said Sir Roger.

"Perhaps an ambush?" suggested de Gresely. "We know the King plans to travel across the Wash from Lynn, surely this is an opportunity for a small band of brave men to waylay him en route? There will be no-one to see, the King might be assumed to have been lost in the marsh, Lord knows the area is treacherous enough!"

"Attack in the marshes? Impossible!" said Sir Roger. "For one thing, there is no concealment for ambush. The tracks only allow single file for horses and to step off the track in armour is to invite certain death in the mud. The area will be as dangerous to us as to the King's men. The King will have a strong force with him, archers and men-at-arms to guard his train. Besides we cannot be sure the King will travel with the baggage train. He may send it on ahead, or take some other route that will provide the luxury more befitting his station."

"We are at impasse then gentlemen," sighed Adam, "will no-one rid us of this troublesome King?"

The room lapsed into thoughtful silence. William sat pondering, his face troubled.

"There is another way," he ventured, "but it is fraught with peril and may even endanger our immortal souls."

"Explain," asked Sir Roger, "at this stage I would sign a deal with the Devil himself! Forgive me Father," he hastily added noting Geoffrey's disapproving scowl.

"I was born and raised in a small village not far from here," William told them, "a remote place on the coast. There was a local woman living out away from the village; she was called *Mother* by the locals. There were many rumours and legends about her. I saw her once, when I was a small boy. The catch had been bad that season, we faced the prospect of a hungry winter. The village elders approached Mother and asked her to perform a certain ritual. This is an old country, gentlemen; before the coming of the Word of Our Lord there were many *old ways* practiced here. Some say there are... others... those who were here before us, who can be turned to for help.

So it was that one day at the water's edge, Mother carried out her pagan ritual. My father took me home, so I saw very little. The catch increased the next day and the following day. In fact, we had an overabundance for many weeks after."

"Well, that's all well and good," interrupted de Gresely, "but how do witches by the sea help our predicament?"

"By this, Milord. The witch, as you call her, may have some method of striking at the King. Many spoke of the curses she used to bring down enemies. There were disappearances at times. If she has access to such powers, then mayhap she can persuaded to help us. Assuming she still lives, of course. She looked old when I was a boy, though many village elders spoke of her being there when they were but children themselves."

"Good God, have we come to this," asked Geoffrey, "shall we turn to pagan devils to do our work?"

"Some might say it is the devil's work," said Simon. "What matter the instrument if the intent be good? Do we condemn the sword for cutting down the disbeliever? The rope for hanging the traitor?"

"Put not your trust in princes, nor in the son of man.... very well," Geoffrey placed his head in his hands "Speak to your witch Brother William, then let us reconvene and make further decision."

The group nodded assent and one by one the conspirators left, furtive and cloaked.

Lutton, The Wash, three days later

Abbot William nudged the donkey along the narrow track. Tall reeds obscured the view to each side and did something to protect him from the chill breeze blowing in off the sea. He had spent the night at Sutton St Mary's, though said nothing of his mission to the clergy there. As far as anyone was concerned he was merely revisiting his boyhood home and family.

The donkey was slow but steady - and steady counted for a lot in this region. A horse that skittered due to a marsh fowl being put up may well run straight into the water - or worse, the mud. Although it was barely mid-morning a low mist already moved across the path. The settlement of Lutton shortly came into view, clinging as it did between the marsh on one side and the sea on the other.

Leaving the donkey in the care of the small tavern, William set off along the beach. Winding his way between fishermen busy at their small boats, he made for the far end of the strand. There he found the track he remembered from his youth, one that as children they dared each other to run along, the one that led to Mother's house. Within seconds, village, fishermen and sea disappeared from view. William found himself winding deeper and deeper into the marshes. Midges and other insects swarmed around him, he grew hot and sticky despite the chill autumn breeze. The atmosphere grew oppressive, there was a dank smell in the air. Strange bird cries sounded every now and then, though William never saw a sign of any bird.

William was almost ready to give up, thinking Mother was no longer alive, when the track opened into a small clearing. A handful of tumbledown shacks ringed the space, patchwork constructions of mud, wattle and old boat timbers. In the centre of the clearing a crudely carved stone pillar thrust skyward.

Nothing moved. William stepped closer to the central stone. It was larger than a man, though quite thin. He made out carvings as he approached it, curious figures, squat, with distorted features. Other lines suggested some form of script, though as William stared at them they seemed to writhe and move slightly. He felt the pull of something beyond his understanding, as though he stood on the gulf of a precipice, where up was down and if he pitched forward he would not fall, but rise... rise through dark, green depths, up towards the distant light.... a light in which were outlined strange silhouettes of creatures swimming above him... beckoning.

"Don't get too close - you may not come back!"

William jerked back, he had gotten much closer to the stone than he thought. He spun round to see a figure framed in the dark doorway of the largest hut. Mother. She was a short yet stocky figure. There was a hint of hidden strength in her posture and movement. She showed no signs of age or infirmity. Shapeless rags concealed much of her and, in many ways, William was grateful for it.

Long, lank hair framed a squat, misshapen face. Large, bulbous eyes surveyed him; they seemed almost to have faint luminous glow in the half light of the shack. A stubby nose in the centre, underlined by a curiously wide mouth, thick lips curled up at one edge in amusement. Mother lifted a flabby, mottled arm and beckoned. "Enter, priest!"

William walked into the hut, though it took some willpower to do so. He felt the touch of unseen eyes from the other shacks.

"Sit!" Mother beckoned to a stool beside a low table. William sat. With an effort he kept his gaze forward and down - he had glimpses of things hanging in the hut that he had no wish to examine closely.

"Speak!" Mother sat opposite him.

"I seek assistance in a difficult task. A means to remove someone that will leave no obvious trace. This person is important and we must take all means in order to-"

"I know of whom you speak," hissed Mother, "I hear all in these parts, especially of those who bring fire and sword into the Fen!"

"Then you sympathise with our cause? You will help rid us of the tyrant?"

Mother cackled, a curious bubbling, wheezing sound. William blanched as her foul breath rode over him.

"Your cause? Your cause? What is your cause to me? You are here and gone quicker than the tide, your lives nothing more than a wave upon the ocean. Those you call Kings are but beggars before the true rulers, swine digging in the mud. Your so-called Kings will come and go and the Old Ones will still remain!"

"What is this blasphemy you speak, our Church and King rule this land, now and forever!" William protested.

Mother laughed once more "Ah, but the future! The future, priest. I have seen it in my dreams! Your abbeys and grand buildings will be ruins... bony fingers pointing to the sky. Your grand knights will burn! Fire and pestilence will sweep your lands, your Kings will be gone, executed by their own kind.... and you speak to me of your cause?"

Mother arose, smiting the table with a heavy fist. Unblinking she leaned towards him, a strange gleam playing in her eyes. "And yet... I shall give you what you require... though there is a price."

"Name it and let me begone from this place," stammered William

"Gold. Jewels. Such trifles can be useful to my kind. The reasons need not concern you."

"The King has gold with him, carried in a baggage train. "

"Then we will take the King's gold."

"But there will be archers, men-at-arms, soldiers, you have none of these here."

Mother sat down and laughed again.

"How ignorant you are. Bring word of the train's whereabouts and the rest shall be arranged."

"Very well.... I agree. Now, can you provide what we need?"

Mother turned to a dark corner of the hut, then placed a small vial on the table.

"This is what you seek. It is a draught that assists with The Change. In large enough dose it will bring a fast and ruinous adjustment to the human body, more than a human can cope with. The body will bloat, the insides will become... different. It will look like no poison known to man."

"Change? What is this change of which you speak?"

Mother cackled again. "You think you are made in your God's image? You are made in *their* image.... or at least from the same clay! You carry *their* seed within you!"

"They? Who are they?"

"The Ones who were here before and will be here long after your kind is gone. For the oceans will rise again! Your kind may tame the seas for a time, but it will be like holding back the waves with sand. All this will again be their domain!"

William shuddered and grabbed the vial. With the speed of a snake, Mother grasped his wrist, in a surprisingly strong grip.

"Would you like me to show you? There are those here undergoing the Change... those born of *them*! "

Mother drew closer, mocking William's look of horror.

"Oh yes priest, for you see your kind has some uses... as breeding stock!"

With a wrench William pulled himself free and ran from the hut. The mocking laughter of Mother followed him as he leant against the rough wall of the hut opposite, trying to compose himself.

A sound made him turn, something moved inside the hut. Through gaps in the wall he caught sight of something large, greyish bulk. Then a large blank eye appeared at the gap, like a yellow, gibbous moon. There was a loud croak as the thing banged on the hut wall, as though seeking to break through to the monk. William took to his heels, running back to the beach as though he were a young man again. Not until he reached the village did he stop, gasping for breath and praying fervently.

Lynn, two days later

Geoffrey de Serland raised his eyebrows to his brother Raymond as they approached the King's chamber. From inside they could hear the King's raised voice.

"I said wine you fool, bring me wine, not this horse piss!" The sound of a goblet being hurled against the wall was followed by the door opening and a flustered serving lad leaving the room at great speed.

The two men entered. King John sat a table, chewing on a joint of meat. As was common these days, he seemed in foul temper. News of the continuing rebellion had just reached him and lent even greater urgency to his plans.

"You, out!" He gestured with the beef bone to a tearful maid who clasped the torn material of her blouse with white-knuckled hands. The wench fled and the King gestured to his bodyguards to be seated.

"Once it is assembled, I'm sending you two with the baggage train across the Wash. The sooner we get everything to Lincoln the better. Savaric and a small group will accompany me; we will travel around the marshes. I'll not spend another day in this hellhole, this damp plays havoc with my joints!"

"Across the marshes sire, is that wise?" ventured Raymond.

"It's a faster route," explained the King, "local guides have been arranged, it will save days of travel and there will be no chance of those damned rebels getting their hand on my treasures!"

The last was shouted and led King John into a coughing fit.

"It is decided! Now, where is that boy with the dammed wine!"

Swineshead Abbey, the next day

"Good tidings my fellows," Abbot Geoffrey addressed the group,"not only has Brother William our poison, but we have received news that the King will be travelling separately from his retinue and baggage train - and he plans to rest here overnight before moving onto Lincoln."

"We have our chance then!" said de Gresely ,"within these walls we can get close!"

"But it still begs the question," pointed out Adam, "how do we administer the dose?"

"I will do it," spoke Simon. "It would not be meet to ask one of the Brothers to do it. I am a soldier, it is my duty to protect my order, by any means necessary. I will disguise myself as a monk and serve the tyrant his last drink."

"And the poison - it will leave no trace?" asked Hugh.

"Oh there will be some effects, but they will appear to be caused by disease rather than poison," said William. "In any case, we plan that Brother Adam will tend to the body as soon as possible and do his best to disguise anything questionable."

"It is decided then," said Sir Roger, "let us pray for success gentlemen!"

"And also for our souls," added Abbot Geoffrey. "Abbot William, I would ask you give absolution to Simon before the deed. He does an evil thing for a good cause and I would have no stain on his soul because of it!"

Abbot William nodded his assent and guided the young Templar knight into the chapel.

Walpole Cross Keys, the next day

Geoffrey de Serland counted the wagons as they passed by him through the narrow street. His brother Raymond ed at the head of the column, alongside the guide, followed by a small group of men-at-arms. Archers were positioned at intervals along the wagons and Geoffrey was to bring up the rear with another group of men-at-arms.

"That's the lot, sir!" said one of the men-at-arms.

"Alright John, I'll ride with you at the back if you think an old bastard like me can keep up."

The grizzled soldier chuckled and spat into the straw at his feet. "Reckon the quicker we get across these marshes the better, looks like fog coming in already!"

The long train set out along the narrow track that led from the town into the marshes. The tread of hooves, the jingle of harness and the low murmur of men were deadened by the surrounding mists. A light drizzle began to fall. Each man spoke quietly to his nearest companion, or remained wrapped in his own thoughts.

At the head of the column, Raymond led his horse by the bridle, keeping close to the guide. The guide was a strange, stunted looking character, but he seemed assured in his step and made no hesitation when coming to forks and branches in the track. The path was narrow and rose above the surrounding marsh in most places. Vegetation was sparse and the dark, shiny mud and brackish water lay on every side as far as the eye could see. As they progressed the fog became thicker still, until Raymond could see scarce ten feet in any direction.

It was close to midday, yet little could be seen of the sun, save a pale hazy glow overhead. Raymond 's horse began to whicker and whine, pulling on the bridle as he led the beast. He heard the same sound from the horses behind him and turned to see if there was any cause for the disturbance.

When he turned back, the guide had vanished! Raymond cursed under his breath - what treachery was this? There was sudden movement in the mud and water around them. Raymond drew his sword "To arms! To arms!" he roared and looked around in vain for an enemy.

The alarm travelled down the column to the rearguard. Geoffrey turned to John beside him - but the old soldier was no longer there, he had gone! Then shapes born of nightmare hove into view.

On all sides, figures rose from the mud and water. Broadly man-like in size and outline, but with features that were in no way human... toad-like faces, bulbous, fish eyes... what seemed like gills along the neck. The creatures were greyish green in colour, with large webbed talons. With a hideous croaking they fell on the baggage train. Sharp claws reaked havoc amongst the surprised men, blood sprayed brightly into the air, men cried out in fear and pain!

Raymond let out a roar as his horse was dragged screaming by two of the creatures, backwards into the water. Soon the stallion was up to its shoulders in the glutinous mud as the devils tore at it. The young knight put all his power into an overhead blow, bringing his sword down the shoulder of the nearest creature. The impact shocked up his arm and with dismay he saw that he had barely made any mark on the beast's tough hide. The creature back-swiped him and Raymond fell heavily to the floor, stunned.

He struggled to his knees, nose pouring blood, as the scene of carnage unfolded around him. The wagon drivers died first, being dragged down and eviscerated in the mud. Blood spayed brightly in the grey gloom. Small knots of men-at-arms stood shoulder to shoulder and attempted to fight the creatures. They were either clawed to pieces, despite their Armour, or dragged off the path and into the sucking mud, where they floundered and drowned. Horses and men screamed in their agonies, the creatures continued their hideous croaking.

Within a matter of minutes, neither man nor horse was left alive. Bodies were pulled off of the path and hurled out into the marsh. Wagons were ripped apart, chests and bags containing the King's treasures carried off by the creatures into the fog, never to be seen again by human eyes.

Swineshead Abbey two days later

The King was in an even fouler temper. There was still no sign of the baggage train, or any of the retinue accompanying it. He had spent the previous day at Wisbech, where the train was due to appear. Now he sat in the abbey refectory, brooding. The grim figure of his bodyguard, Sir Savaric de Mauleon, loomed behind him, always close at hand.

"God's wounds can no-one tell me what is going on?" The assembled monks flinched at the King's outburst.

"Our messengers have returned milord," Abbot William ventured, "none have seen any sight of the train after it left Lynn. There are but few ways in and out of the marshes; we fear the whole train may have been lost. It is a very treacherous place."

"Treacherous? Treacherous? You speak to me of treachery, you mealy mouthed priests! Don't think I am ignorant of your conniving, your plotting, you're lucky I don't have you all put to death!"

At this Savaric's hand moved to the hilt of his broadsword. Abbot William swallowed hard.

"I assure Milord, we have only his best interests at heart."

"Bring me food and drink! And that pretty little wench I saw on the way in - send her to my chambers later!"

"But milord that is Sister Judith - not only is she my own sister, but she is a Bride of Christ!" William looked horrified.

"Do you defy me monk? Deliver her to my chamber this night, or your head will be on a spike over your main gate, do you understand? Drink, man! Food!"

Abbot William rushed from the room to the kitchens. Simon was there waiting, dressed in the white robes of the order.

"It is time," the Abbot said to the young Templar.

"I'm ready father," Simon poured the potion into a large goblet of cider, "and Gold help us all."

The food was carried in on platters and Simon followed with the goblet. The food was laid out in front of the King.

"About time!" he shouted. Simon approached with the

goblet and, bowing his head, proffered it to the King.

"Hmmm..." the King glanced up at the disguised Templar, then at the goblet.

"Taste it!"

"Pardon milord?" Simon asked in a querulous voice.

"You heard me... taste it! My taster is with the train.... you are here. So taste it!"

Simon looked around the room. Abbot William stood still as a statue, perhaps offering some internal prayer. Savaric's hand once again moved to his sword hilt. Simon lifted the jewelled goblet to his lips and took a draught. There was no indication in taste of the presence of the witch's potion. Simon lowered the goblet. All eyes were on him. For what seemed like an eternity the King said nothing. Then he snatched the goblet out of Simon's hand.

"On your way, boy!" he snarled, before taking a deep draught of the cider. Simon, afraid that his legs would buckle under him, bowed and slowly walked out of the chamber. The Abbot followed. The young man leant against the wall in the corridor and exhaled heavily.

"I confess father, I have faced fanatical men in battle, but nothing filled me with as much fear as that moment!"

"You did well my son. Now, we just have to wait. In the meantime I will advise Sister Judith to leave immediately, in case our plans go awry."

It was an hour later, after the King had retired to his private chamber, that there was first indication of success. Savaric appeared, summoning the Abbot to the King's side. When the Abbot entered the chamber, the King was lying on the bed in considerable distress. His face was grey and clammy, his breath foul.

"Have you a physician here Abbot?" the bodyguard asked?

William nodded and sent for one of the monks. He arrived and set about examining the King, who complained vociferously at every prod and turn.

"I fear the King has a fever and some ailment of the digestion," the monk reported. "I suggest he rest here for the night."

"Rest be dammed," the King hissed through clenched lips "I must away to Lincoln!" He attempted to rise, then clutching his stomach fell back on the bed.

"If I might suggest milord rest here the night, then travel on to Lincoln tomorrow?" Abbot William offered.

The King nodded and waved a hand in dismissal. Abbot William exited the room, going straight to see Simon.

"It has worked, the potion has taken hold! According to Mother it will take a day or two to do its work. Well done Simon, you may have saved us all. Now, I suggest you leave quickly, lest any suspicions be aroused and we are questioned."

Simon nodded, "I shall return to the preceptory at Temple Bruer and await further news."

The next morning the King's entourage prepared to leave Swineshead Abbey. The King was carried, slumped between two courtiers and placed into his carriage. Without a glance at the Abbot and assembled monks, he waved the group on, his bodyguard flanking him on a great charger. It was the last they ever saw of the King.

Tower Bruer Templar Preceptory, 29th October 1216

"I'm sure you know the rest, Father Thomas," the cowled figure concluded. "The King arrived at Lincoln castle, then died the next day. Of course, we had made sure that Abbot

Adam was in place to attend to the body. The few servants
with the King had already fled it seemed, after looting his
belongings. The bodyguard was gone too. Adam prepared the
body as best he could, though by all accounts there had been
considerable changes to the Kings appearance. That may have
worked in our favour, as it seems none were keen to closely
examine a diseased corpse.

In any case, Brother Adam did his best and the King's
corpse was packed and sent down to London for burial. None
has come forward to challenge anything; as far as all are
concerned the King died of some natural malady. The way is
now clear for the Dauphin, let the dice fall where they may."

The hooded figure paused and sat back, as if some load had
been lifted from him.

"I understand my son." Thomas assured him. "I'm sure we
are all glad to be rid of the tyrant." Then he asked the
question that was to haunt him for the rest of his days.

"But one thing puzzles me. You recounted in your tale, how
Abbot William granted you absolution for the deed you were
about to do. Why now do you seek absolution again for that
deed?"

The figure opposite him laughed, an unpleasant, croaking
sound that carried no humour in it.

"Oh no, you see Father I don't seek absolution for what I
have done. I seek absolution for what I am going to do.... and
what I am going to become. For I drank of the potion, Father.
Not a great amount, but I drank of it nonetheless."

"I don't understand, surely the potion was fatal only in
large doses?"

"Fatal yes. But in smaller doses, it brings about change, and
already there have been changes. They are quickening too. So

you see, Father, I can no longer remain here, I can longer be part of this Order. You must pray for what little remains of my soul Father, for shortly I shall be with *them*. I shall be of *them* and at one with *them*. I understand now where we are from and I confess,Father, that while part of me abhors this change another part of me welcomes it, in fact revels in it. But here, let me show you..."

With that the figure lifted its hands to the cowl. The sleeves of the robe fell a little, exposing grey, rough-skinned arms. Simon pulled back the hood and Thomas screamed, as he looked into the ocean-spawned features of a man that was no longer a man.

Remnants

YOU HAUNT ME

icture a house. Not a grand place, but not a hovel. Not totally run down, but it has seen better days. A large cottage, dark slate roof, light grey walls. It stands alone on the edge of a field at the end of a track. Trees border the house on three sides, gently nodding in the night breeze. Around, all is dark. Dark earth, dark sky, even the nearby dyke water is dark and still.

There is a light in a window, a small beacon in the surrounding gloom. It is the only light visible for miles, there is no moon outside, just the dark. All other windows are empty and black. We move in closer to the window and can make out the shape of a man's face through the thick glass.

The man sits in a high backed armchair. Before him, on a small table, stands a candle, the source of the light. The rest of the room is in shadow, as though the man exists only in this bubble of light. The man holds a glass in his hand from which he occasionally sips. He looks troubled. This is the only room in the house he can use now, she has all the rest.

The house used to be bright. Filled with laughter and light. The happy young couple, the thrill of a first home, the prospect of a long life together, children, happiness and tears shared. Now there is only the dark.

It started when she went. Disappeared. Questions were asked of course, investigations made. Some of her things were gone, a suitcase missing. Relatives were visited, enquiries made. There were hints of a lover, of unhappiness in the home. There were no close neighbours to question, but in such isolated communities it is difficult to keep secrets.

Nothing was ever found. She seemed to have disappeared off the face of the earth. Searches were planned, but where to start? The wide open fields, criss-crossed with narrow, deep dykes? The dark, wide river perhaps, enclosed in its high banks? Maybe the nearby marshland, so treacherous to the unwary. Attempts were made, dogs brought in, but no-one held any real hope. And so eventually the investigators moved on to other, more urgent cases. The file remained open but was placed in the archives. She was gone.

The man thought so too. He was sure she had gone. Yet things began to happen. Small things at first. Every couple of weeks he would visit the nearby village for supplies. He was not unaware of the looks he got, or the whispers, the mothers who quickly pulled their children away. He didn't care, why should he? But he did care when, walking across the village green, he heard her call his name. Just the once it came, his name hanging in the air like an echo. He spun around, but she was not there.

It started to happen every time he went to the village - so he stopped going. Stocked up on food, he could stay in the house for months. And so summer passed into autumn, into winter. The dark earth lay blanketed in snow, white as far as the eye could see, merging into the heavy grey sky in the distance.

The man's breath hung like great clouds of steam as he broke the ice on the water barrel. On an impulse he stepped to the small gate and glanced over it down the long track. It was invisible beneath the snow, soft, untouched - but no! There, clear in the crisp morning air…. tracks… footprints… her footprints! After that he stopped going out of the house.

And then sometimes, coming into the bedroom he caught a trace of her perfume. It grew stronger each time too, and masked some other scent, something more foul. It grew so strong that in time the man stopped using the bedroom.

There was the mirror too. The man was shaving one day - well you have to keep up standards - when he caught a glimpse in the mirror of her face. Just for an instant - her face! The man jumped, nicking his skin with the frosty razor. Bright red blood drops pitter-pattered onto the cold white porcelain. The man turned to see.... nothing. So the man stopped using the bathroom.

Downstairs was comfortable enough. The range in the kitchen, the fire in the sitting room, the armchair to sleep in. Until that night in the kitchen! Preparing some soup he happened to glance up and out of the window. There she was! The snow reflected moonlight bathed her in an icy glow. Standing stock still, like a frozen statue, face down and hidden by her long black hair. With a cry the man jumped back, dropping the soup with a clatter. After that he stopped using the kitchen.

Now he sits in his armchair, the candle flame is the room's sole illumination. Even the fire has gone out; the only source of warmth the fierce spirit on which he sips. All is silent apart from the slow, heavy ticking of the clock. Then a slight sound brings him out of his reverie. Something small rolls across the table towards him and stops, shining in the candlelight. It is an earring, one of a pair he bought her not long after they'd met. He knows she can't be here though. He knows she is gone... because he helped her to go.

The clock stops. A pale face moves into the candle light. Bone white, the eyes are dark pits with no flicker of life within. The lips are pulled back over yellowed teeth. Livid blue marks contrast with the white skin on the neck. A terrible face... her face. She leans forward and with a single, rattling sigh blows out the candle...

WILLOW DROVE END

The wide grey sky.... slow moving clouds reflected in shining, still pools.. .a faint breeze touches my face, bringing with it the smell of...the sea? Maybe... but something else too. Decay,rot. There is no sound, no bird song, no piercing gull cry. No sign of life.... and yet I feel I am being watched. Someone or something knows I am here. Could it be her? I close the car door and begin a slow walk along the narrow path. That smell again, carried on the sea breeze. It takes me back sharply to that day over forty years ago, the first time I smelled it.

◆

Fourteen is an awkward age to go on holiday with your parents. Too old for candy floss and sandcastles, too young to be home alone. The drive up from London wasn't much fun, crammed into Uncle Trevor's car along with Auntie Jean and Mum and Dad.

Not for us the allure of foreign climes and sun kissed beaches. No, this was the early 70's and times were hard. We were heading to a caravan site on the East coast, at the recommendation of Uncle Trev.

"I've been there a few times, it's great," he explained, "in fact I took your dad there for his stag do - back before you were even a tadpole!" he laughed.

Through the steamed-up glass I saw the road change from motorway to A road to B road and eventually to not much more than a sandy track. The scenery likewise changed, the urban sprawl of North East London long gone, replaced by the wide, open expanses of the Fens. Then there was the huddle of village houses before turning off onto a narrow, raised road, Willow Drove, who's shiny, grey surface stretched off into the fog. After a long, bumpy ride we reached a huddle of shabby buildings then, following a sign, turned off into a car park. We got out and surveyed our holiday paradise.

The smell was the first thing that struck me. Ozone and sea, underpinned with something else.... rotten seaweed? Maybe it was just the smell of the mudflats that stretched around us. The small car park overlooked an area of built up land which had a couple of dozen caravans stood on it, along with a toilet block and what looked like some kind of club house, all slatted wood and shuttered windows.

"Well this is...nice,"said Mum. Aunty Jean said nothing; she was quiet at the best of times. Dad and Uncle Trevor began getting the cases out of the back of the car as a figure appeared out of the mist.

"Afternoon!" he exclaimed. "I'm Doug Orne, the site manager. Welcome to Willow Drove End Caravan Site!" He nodded to the two men, glanced briefly at me, then settled his gaze on Mum and Aunty Jean.

"I hope you have a lovely time."

He grinned, showing tobacco-stained teeth, touched the brim of his tatty old hat and beckoned.

"Come into the office, lets get you booked in!"

Ten minutes later we were sat in one of the parks "luxury" caravans with the kettle on the boil. The smell was still there, fainter, but there. The caravan felt cold and slightly damp, the fittings and fixtures basic. Mum was not impressed. Uncle Trevor seemed in better spirits, whispering and nudging Dad like they had some private joke. Dad seemed uneasy but was laughing along nonetheless.

"I'll get some lunch on," said Mum. "Charlie why don't you

have a look round the site, perhaps you'll find some new
friends! Be back in half an hour, love."
I zipped up my bomber jacket and went back outside. Where
to start - everywhere looked grey, everywhere looked flat. I
headed towards the clubhouse. It was all locked up apart
from a small side room that had a couple of pinball tables and
a Pong machine beeping away. Outside was a sign that
pointed *Beach* one way and *Shop* another. I opted for the
latter and followed the path back towards the village.

After a few minutes I found the shop. There was a display
rack of paperbacks outside, plus some beach balls, footballs
and an inflated lilo. I picked one of the paperbacks and went
in, pushing aside the shell curtain in the doorway. There was
a lady with two kids at the counter, talking to the woman at
the till. As I came in they stopped talking and turned to look
at me. I must have jumped a bit, the woman's face took me by
surprise. She had long greasy hair and a pale, pinched face.
Her lips were drawn back in a kind of grimace, revealing
stubby teeth. Her look was one of pure venom. The two girls
with her looked similar, maybe they were twins. They had a
kind of vacant look, as though they didn't even really see me.
The mother grabbed her two girls and rushed them out of the
shop, the shells clattering in their wake.

"Help you duck?" asked the lady behind the counter. She at
least looked normal.

"I'd like this book, please - oh and a Caramac"

The lady passed the bar to me, "That will be 45 pence, dear"

I handed over a 50 pence piece. It was as she handed me
back my change that I noticed her hand - or to be more
specific the slight webbing between the fingers. I stammered
quick thanks before getting out of there quick. I tucked the
book in my jacket pocket and headed back to the site.

This time, I followed the sign for the beach. Another narrow sandy track led up and over a low rise. Steps on the other side led down to what was optimistically called "the beach". Some small dunes, a ribbon of sand and then mud... grey, shiny mud. The sea was a distant silver strip. The place was empty apart from a group of people about a hundred yards away, huddled in the lee of a windbreak, drinking from a thermos. I sat down in the dunes and broke out the Caramac.

"Shit, this is going to be a long week."

Any doubts I had about the lack of thrills for the week ahead were only confirmed that night in the clubhouse. Us and about six other family groups sat at the formica tables, under the buzzing fluorescent lights. Most of the men stood at the bar nursing pints, while a young kid ran up and down, knee-sliding on the dance floor. Manager Doug - now "Uncle Doug", resplendent in a red, frilly shirt - manned a DJ console at the end of the room and was playing last year's Top Twenty hits, interspersed with witty banter in a mid-Atlantic accent.

Two pints of lemonade in and I needed a break, not to mention a pee. The club room was stuffy, smoky and hot, so after a pee I went outside to get some air. I heard voices from round the corner of the building - one was Dad's. Something made me stop, instead of saying anything I sidled quietly up to the corner and listened.

"Come on Al," it was Uncle Trevor. "You remember how much fun we had on your stag do!"

"That was different Trev, it was years ago. Anyway you got me so pissed I didn't know what I was doing. In fact, I don't remember much of it at all!" Dad replied.

"I remember that number you cracked of with," Uncle

Trevor laughed. "Gawd, what a sight! She virtually dragged you off by your hair, after an hour or so we were thinking of sending a rescue party!"

"All I remember is waking up in the dunes with a shitty hangover," Dad mumbled. "But I don't suppose that stopped you having your fun, did it Trev?"

Uncle Trevor's voice seemed tense and angry in reply.

"Each to their own Al! Anyway, even if you're not up for some fun I still am. For now, let's get back before the women start wondering where we are. I'm sure Jean will be wanting another Babycham."

I turned and headed quickly back inside, where the bingo was in full flow.

The next couple of days passed slowly. We were mostly sat on the beach, or eating and playing cards in the caravan. Evenings were spent in the clubhouse that smelt increasingly of stale fags and beer. But that other smell that I noticed on first arriving was still there.. faint, but there.

It was on the third evening that things changed. After an hour in the clubhouse and the looming prospect of something called a "meat raffle", I decided that anything was better than this. I headed out of the clubhouse, my hand in my pocket grasping the pack of Benson and Hedges I managed to half inch off the bar earlier. I headed for the beach, lighting one of the fags on the way.

Over the dunes, the beach was deserted. A slight breeze cooled the humid night air. The smell of sea and rot was heavy here. The water was closer in, lapping softly at the sand. I walked along the beach, the glow from my cigarette the only light apart from the pale sliver of moon. I walked to the far end of the beach - I hadn't been up this far before, we were of the type who, once they have a spot on the beach, return to it every single time.

I noticed a track leading off through the dunes. Throwing the finished butt aside I continued. The path twisted through the dunes, went over a small bank and then finished in a clearing. The sandy space was ringed by short, thorny trees and some thick bushes. It seemed odd to have a path that led nowhere. I was about to turn back when I heard a sound, the low mutter of voices through the trees.

Following the sound, I found a small opening in the vegetation, only around four feet high. I ducked down and went through. A couple of thorny branches snagged on my jacket, but twisting, I managed to free myself. The sandy track continued on the other side. I could see a large shape up ahead and the murmurs were louder. For some reason I was overcome with a feeling of caution - something wasn't right here. I moved to the edge of the track, where the trees were thinner and offered cover without stopping movement. Crouching down, I moved forward and to the right, aiming to circle round whatever was ahead and come in at a different angle.

The large shape resolved itself into a caravan. I was approaching it from the rear corner. At the front, gathered around the door I could see a group of fthree men. Locals, judging from their clothes and accents. Their faces were lit by the glow of cigarettes, their voices low, their body language furtive. I moved in close to the caravan. There was a noise coming from inside, a rhythmic creak. The large window at the end was slightly open, I carefully peeked in, ready to duck down out of sight if need be.

The interior was filled with shadow, the only light came from a small lamp. There was a smell of stale tobacco, unwashed bodies and... that sea smell again. A figure was on the narrow bed, a large man, his back to me. I couldn't see his face, he was face down, hips rising and falling - the source of the creaking. He grunted and moaned, then arched his back, bringing his head up and back.

It was then I saw the girl. Underneath him, dwarfed by his bulk. She looked barely older than me. I could see little more than her pale face, it was blank and expressionless. But then it happened. I don't how she knew I was there... but she turned and looked directly at me. Those eyes – bulging, shining. They locked onto mine and I couldn't look away. She saw me... I mean saw me completely. There was a strange look in those eyes. There was a pleading, there was pain, but there was also something triumphant, something defiant. And most of all there was a look of recognition, as though she knew me.

I don't know how long I stood there transfixed, but at some point I fell back, in a cold sweat. I didn't know how to process this information. My first instinct was to get out of there. I began creeping back the way I had come in. I heard the caravan door open and close behind me and the men's low laughter.

I got back through the gap and into the clearing and was about to head back along the path, when I heard voices approaching from the beach. With nowhere to go I shrugged back into the shadowy branches, ignoring the thorns that bit at my flesh. Two figures appeared in the clearing, silhouetted as they came over the bank. Uncle Trevor and Doug.

"Same arrangement as before then?" I heard Uncle Trevor ask

"That's right, though I've got something new for you this time." replied Doug

Uncle Trevor reached into his pocket and handed over what

looked like a roll of notes to Doug.

"But is it what I like Doug - you know my tastes," he said.

"Oh yes," Doug replied, "it's just what you like."

"And her parents?"

"Don't worry. Father not around and mother, well, she went back to her folks last year. The girl was put into my charge. Now then," as they squeezed through the small gap, "move off you men, there's a valued customer coming through!"

The clearing was empty, but the prospect of the locals coming back through it got my feet moving. I was up and along the path, back along the beach. I didn't stop until I reached the clubhouse, regretting that earlier fag as I coughed and spluttered, holding on to the wall for support.

"What's up with you, sport?" Dad's voice brought me round from my spasms.

"Nothing Dad, just a bit of a coughing fit."

"Yeah well, fags will do that to you - don't think I didn't notice!" I must have looked alarmed.

"Don't worry, I won't tell your mum. Come on, I'll buy you a bag of pork scratching." Dad laughed and ruffled my head "You don't want to be hanging round out here."

Sleep that night came quickly but was troubled with dreams. I dreamt of falling, of being smothered, then of sinking in cold, dark water.... but through the gloom I saw those eyes, and a pale hand reaching out to mine.... pulling me up and towards safety.....

I awoke with a start, to raised voices. It was Mum.

"I don't care Alan, I'm not putting up with it anymore and I want us to leave - now!"

"Come on love, " Dad replied. "Let's make the best of it, it's only a few more days!"

"No! I'm packing, we are going now! Charlie," Mum had turned and saw me sitting up. "Get dressed, get packed, we're leaving!"

Half an hour later the three of us we were climbing into a minicab. Uncle Trevor was stood in the caravan door, arms crossed, scowling. Aunty Jean was by the car. Mum hugged her and kissed her on the cheek.

"You can come with us Jean," she said, "no one would blame you."

"No," said Aunty Jean, "I'll stay. It's.... well he is what he is."

We were in the cab and away, my last sight out of the rear window was Auntie Jean stood stock still, staring at the receding car, Uncle Trevor stepping behind her and putting his hands on her shoulders.

◆

There's not much more to tell. I never saw Uncle Trevor again. He killed himself a few years later, hosepipe and exhaust job from what I heard. We didn't go to the funeral. Aunty Jean went back up to her family in Scotland.

As for me, I did the usual stuff. Grew up, got a job, got married to Julie, we had a kid of our own, Samantha, a lovely girl.

The dreams never left me though. In fact, over time they got worse. Always the same - the suffocation, a feeling of being crushed, paralysis. Water closing in over my head... sinking.... screaming for help.... the cold water filling my nose, my mouth, my lungs. Sharp pains in the chest, lungs bursting. And then that face, those eyes, the cold hand in mine, pulling me towards the light., before bursting awake, shouting and soaked in sweat.

I found the only way to stop the dreams was to self-medicate. Sleeping pills were no good. Scotch helped, or vodka. That led to other problems, of course, and eventually Julie left me. Later, after her mum was killed in a car crash, my Sammy moved to Canada to train as a nurse. I've had no contact with her since.

When my scan result came back last month it was almost a relief - now I really did have something to feel sorry about. But it also gave me a focus that I've not had for years. Part of that was getting in touch with old friends and places - and there was one place I saved until last. It wasn't until this morning that I returned to Willow Drove End.

The drive was much the same, though the weather was worse, a cold, grey December day. Turning off the A17 and onto the small B roads, I noticed how much new housing was around. The village itself, at the end of the seemingly endless drove, had grown. New-build estates huddled round what remained of the old wooden slat buildings; a shiny new mini-mart shone brightly in the gloom, there was even a fast food restaurant. I had to search around a bit to find the track that led up to the caravan site. In fact I only noticed it when I caught sight of a damp, twisted and mildewed sign - *Willow Drove End Caravan Park.*

I edged the car along the track and into the car park. The mist was here again, the sea smell heavy on the air. The clubhouse, though, was a derelict ruin. No sign of any caravans, just forty years of undergrowth. I left the car and headed up the sandy track, still visible, up over the dyke and down to the beach. Here, there was no change. Through the sparse dunes, onto the slim strand of sand. The mudflats beyond stretched off into the mist. The screech of a gull pierced the gloom, I was totally alone on the edge of the world.

I made my way to the far end of the beach and onto the narrow track. The clearing was still there, though with some rubbish scattered around; an old car seat, some burnt stuff. The narrow gap through the trees was overgrown. It took some time and persistence to force a way through, by which time I was bleeding from several small cuts to my hands.

The caravan squatted there, like some prehistoric monument. The windows were empty, the door hung off a hinge. Furniture from inside had been strewn out and around the doorway. The sides of the caravan were tinged with green mould and mildew, it smelt dank and rotten. Looking inside, the interior was full of filth and rot. A large fungus was growing in the centre of the floor. Some kind of insect scuttled across the worktop as I peered in. The stench was overpowering.

I staggered back into the clearing, then returned to the beach. Even the sea-rot smell here was a relief after the caravan interior. I don't know what I expected, exactly.

But as I stand here on the beach now, something is clear to me. Behind me is my old life, it offers nothing but rot and decay. In front of me, across the mud flats, she is waiting. Just a short, slow, sucking walk across the mud, then the cold still waters will envelop me and she will be there to greet me.... after all, she is the only family I have left.

THE BUTTERLY COLLECTOR

"**S**plendid, splendid, do come in!"

Farnsworth ushered us into the hallway of his Pall Mall residence, closing the heavy door against the winter chill. The ever attentive Ashton collected coats, hats and scarves and we were soon seated comfortably and enjoying a most welcome and hearty repast.

As was his custom, Farnsworth said little or nothing during the meal and it was down to Longhurst, Plympton and myself to fuel the over-dinner conversation. Talk was mostly of current business affairs, a dash of domestic politics and, of course, the usual catch-up gossip of friends who have not enjoyed each others company for a measure of weeks.

Custom continued, with postprandial brandies in Farnsworth's study. The man himself stood stuffing his pipe, one elbow rested on the mantel, enjoying the warmth of the open fire. The rest of us took our cue, settling into the leather chairs, while Ashton circulated with a box of fine cigars.

"Well now," Farnsworth beamed. "What I have to relate tonight was a queer do and no mistake. It concerns a chap, a colleague of mine in fact, called Stiles. A bright enough fellow, the quiet, studious type. There is certainly nothing of the adventure-seeker or *fantastique* about him.

Stiles lectures in Chemistry and is usually to be found wandering round in a lab coat carrying various test tubes and beakers. I wouldn't say he was a close acquaintance but we had chatted a few times and he always seemed a cheerful and polite enough fellow to me.

It was a few weeks ago that I bumped into him - or he bumped into me, rather. I was just tidying my notes after a lecture on the Icelandic Sagas when Stiles appeared at my side and jostled my elbow. He asked if he could have a word, and so, a few minutes later we were up in my rooms nursing a sherry. Stiles had heard of my interest in things unexplained and mysterious, you see. Things that, he admitted, he once thought of as primitive, unscientific and superstitious nonsense.

'There's no place for ghosts in a test tube!' as he put it. I enquired as to whether something had occurred to change his point of view and he sat and told me of a particular experience that occurred over the summer break. See what you think...."

◆

Stiles carefully lifted the case containing his equipment from the overhead rack and, carrying it along with his regular suitcase, disembarked the train at Hoveton. The Norfolk station was small but tidy and, as previously arranged in his correspondence, there was a horse and buggy awaiting him just outside the station entrance. Following a short drive through the pleasant summer countryside, Stiles arrived at The White Horse Inn, his base of operations over the next couple of weeks.

While he was a chemist by vocation, Stiles' other passion was lepidoptery. A keen collector since boyhood, his rooms at Cambridge were filled with many display cases of butterflies alongside his scientific books and journals. His holiday plan was to have a break away from the lab and go spotting and collecting in the Broads. From the Inn Stiles could strike out to nearby Catfield Fen, a place most highly recommended in the esteemed publication *The Entomologist's Record*, to which he was a subscriber.

The efficient and welcoming landlady, Mrs Calthorpe,

showed Stiles to his room, then bustled about straightening pillows and opening curtains before leaving him alone. The room was agreeable, with a most pleasing view across the broads from the wide window. A small desk sat under the window, where Stiles would be able to sit and catalogue his finds. He unpacked his various jars, trays and other such items before going downstairs for a perfectly satisfying, if rather plain, meal in the dining room.

The next morning saw Stiles making an early start. He had made previous arrangements with Mrs Calthorpe to hire a bicycle, which he now set out on, armed with map, sandwiches and the tools of his trade. Even this early in the day it was rather warm and the hum of bees and other insects made a pleasant background drone to the soft breeze and rustle of the reeds. After referring to his map a couple of times, Stiles duly arrived at Catfield Fen and began to survey the area.

It seemed typical enough. Narrow waterways, enclosed by reeds the height of a man in places. Here and there were openings of narrow trails, that presumably led one across and through the Fen. Birdlife abounded. A marsh harrier hovered overhead and Stiles could hear several types of birdsong, along with the honking of an agitated mallard. The hum of insects was louder here and swallowtails and dragonfly fluttered in and out of the vegetation. In fact, the whole place, while appearing rather away from it all and desolate was, in all actuality, teeming with life and activity.

Stiles spent the day exploring the edge of the Fen and searching for any rare butterflies. In that respect he had little success – an abundance of swallowtails, the common blue, the dark green fritillary, but nothing more interesting. Undeterred, in late afternoon he set off back to the Inn.

There were two other guests for dinner that night. Stiles, whilst not normally a sociable fellow, found himself, in the circumstances, forced into conversation. Major and Mrs Deverell holidayed every year in the Broads since retirement, they told him. They had a small boat, on which they journeyed around the waterways, stopping over, here and there, at inns such as this one for two or three nights .

The Major seemed rather disturbed that Stiles was out and about on his own.

"Don't be fooled, the Broads can be a dangerous place! One foot wrong and you're gone forever, what!" he warned.

"Oh yes,"Mrs Deverell interjected, "and don't forget, young man, all those local tales of devil dogs, not to mention the will-o-wisps and fairy lights, luring the unwary traveller to a watery doom!"

Stiles snorted, at which the Major looked slightly offended.

"You may laugh old chap, but when you've seen some of the things we've seen! Why I remember one time at the Shaniwarwada Fort in Poona, there was this-"

"Henry, this is not the time or place," interrupted Mrs Deverell, laying a hand on her husband's arm.

"Hmm well yes - in any case just you be careful, young man, that's all!"

Stiles assured the couple he would take the greatest care and, with nods and thanks, retired for the night.

Having made preliminary investigations, on the second day Stiles resolved to explore deeper into the Fen. After all, the rarest sightings were likely to be in the less accessible places. Taking one of the small track openings at random, he was, within a short time, immersed in a landscape that lay unchanged for centuries. The air was hot and still, midges and all manner of insect filled the heavy air. Stiles was totally enclosed by the reeds and vegetation, with no view to the sides and precious little ahead or behind.

Gradually he worked his way into the heart of the Fen. After a small while he came upon a clearing of sorts. The track here was bisected at right angles by another. In the centre of the clearing, right where the tracks crossed, stood an old stone. About three feet high it stood, slightly angled and weather-worn. There was no inscription or marking on it as far as Stiles could see. Perhaps it was a relic of some old building, or, more likely, a marker or way finder put here by the fen-dwellers of old.

Taking the opportunity for a break, Stiles placed his net on the ground and took the equipment case off of his shoulder. He then sat down to eat his sandwiches and take a swig or two from his flask. Leaning with his back to the stone, the warm sun on his face, the gentle drone of insects surrounding him, Stiles felt his eyelids grow heavy.

He awoke with something of a start. The insect drone had stopped. All was quiet and still. Not even a breeze stirred the rushes. Stiles slowly stood and yawned, then looked behind him.... and there it was!

Sat atop the stone, in all its colourful glory.... a *Large Copper*! Bright and shiny as a new penny! With a sharp intake of breath, Stiles froze. This was a prize indeed, *Lycaena dispar* were thought extinct and it was not that long ago a sample fetched £200 at auction! Without taking his gaze from the butterfly, he reached slowly for the net. His fingers closed around the handle and he began to slowly lift, edging carefully forward. The net came up, inch by inch, to chest height. Then, just as he was about to make his move, the butterfly flew up and away!

Stiles scowled and, quickly grabbing his equipment case, set off in pursuit. The butterfly took the left hand turn, fluttering just ahead of him at head height. Stiles followed as swiftly as he could, but his quarry always seemed just out of reach. Soon he was panting with exertion, the heavy case banging against his hip, the sweat running into his eyes. The old track twisted and turned, the butterfly always remaining frustratingly just out of reach.

With a sudden splash, Stiles found himself knee deep in water. The track had ended abruptly and Stiles now stood at the edge of a large mere. The black, still water was covered here and there with a film of garish, green weed. The whole thing was about fifty feet across as far as Stiles could see. In the centre, a stone construction arose from the mere. It was some kind of small tower, slightly conical in shape. There was an arched opening at the bottom and other, smaller openings higher up. If the large opening was a doorway, the water looked to be about three feet deep, but Stiles had no way of knowing for sure. The butterfly, oblivious to the change in terrain, fluttered across the brackish water and disappeared into the shadow filled, open doorway.

Stiles stood stock still, taking in the surroundings. Could he wade across to the tower? The water may be shallow. On the other hand, there could be hidden depths - not to mention the mud, strong enough to drag a man under in some places he had heard. Discretion got the better part of valour and Stiles decided on a tactical retreat, to return tomorrow better equipped. Stepping back onto the track, he followed it back to the stone marker, boots oozing black mud at every step.

Later that evening, over dinner, he relayed the day's adventures to the Major and his wife. They listened attentively, though when he came to describe the mere and the tower there was a loud crash from behind. The serving girl had the dropped her tray. Crockery smashed and cutlery tinkled on the stone floor. Mrs Calthorpe immediately swept into action, shooing the red-faced girl away, organising a cleanup operation and profusely apologising to the diners.

"I do beg your pardon, daft girl don't know if she's coming or going!"
"Oh don't worry Mrs C, " said the Major.. "No harm done, accidents will happen!"

The rest of the meal passed in peace and, bidding his fellow guests good evening, Stiles made for the stairs. As he placed his hand on the rail, his arm was grabbed. He turned to see Mrs Calthorpe at his side.

"Begging pardon, sir, I overheard earlier you mentioned the old tower in the mere. Well if you don't mind me saying so, I'd give such a place a miss ,if I were you. Those old structures can be very... unsafe. If anything happened to you out there, sir, why no-one would know of it!"

"Thank you for your concern, Mrs Calthorpe, I shall take it under advisement. However I plan to return to the spot tomorrow, one does not ignore the prospect of bagging a *Lycaena dispar*!"

"As you wish sir. Well, I'll bid you goodnight then."

Stiles ascended to his room and retired. After reading for a short while he turned out the light and settled into a deep sleep.

He wasn't sure what awoke him. It felt like the soft brush of something against his face. Sitting up, he could see nothing. Then came a sound... The soft fluttering of something in a dark corner of the room. Not loud, but persistent. There it was again. Stiles rose and moved towards it. But the sound now changed... it was outside, as though something were tapping softly against the window. Stiles moved to the heavy curtains and took hold as if to open them.

For some inexplicable reason, he was overcome with an overwhelming sense of dread. His hands gripped the thick drapes tightly, knuckles bony white in the gloom, but Stiles felt that on no account could he draw the curtains apart! The fluttering and tapping grew louder, more insistent. Stiles trembled, his shoulders shaking with the tension of gripping the curtains. But still he remained in the clutches of this strange, blind panic and couldn't bring himself to open them and reveal the source of the noise.

With a cry, Stiles fell back and the fluttering sound immediately stopped. Shaken, he switched on the light and took a sip of water from the glass on the bedside cabinet. All was at it should be. All was quiet except for the ticking clock and the distant barking of a dog. Stiles returned to his bed, persuading himself the whole thing must have been some kind of nightmare, or half-awake hallucination. Too much sun perhaps? Switching off the light he soon fell again into a deep sleep.

By ten the next morning Stiles was back at the cross-roads and stone marker. This time he was equipped with a pair of waders and a stout pole, courtesy of one the locals back at the village. The Major had waved him off as he and his wife readied their provisions for the day ahead.

Having made his preparations, Stiles plunged determinedly into the Fen and was soon at the crossroads. All was as it had been on the previous day and Stiles took a minute to ready his net. As he did so, the Large Copper appeared again - on

the stone marker, then up and fluttering ahead of him! Once
more, Stiles tried repeatedly without success to net the
butterfly, it always remained just out of his reach! He
followed his elusive prey along the track again, though this
time he was ready for the pool. Instead of a splash, there was
a quiet plop as Stiles lowered both waders into the dark
water.

A single, languid ripple set off across the surface of the
water towards the tower at its centre, following in the wake
of the butterfly, which once more flew into the darkened
doorway. With the net stowed across his shoulders and the
pole firmly grasped in hand, Stiles began his slow walk across
the mere.

Sounding the water in front of him, Stiles edged step by
step towards the tower. Despite the hot sun the water felt icy
cold against his legs. It was thigh deep now. It quickly became
a struggle to lift his feet, the mud pulling at him, making each
step an effort.

The tower loomed closer. From this distance, Stiles could
see how the old stone was blackened, covered in moss and
fungal growth in places. There were no insects, no sounds of
birdsong. All was quiet, save for Stiles laboured breathing
and the soft lapping of the ripples he made. The water was
hip deep now, but he was within about fifteen feet of the
tower. The ground underfoot felt a little firmer here and
seemed to be sloping up slightly. He guessed the tower must
stand on some small rise or island, no doubt above water-
level when it was built.

With firmer going and the upward slope, Stiles found the
last part of the approach much easier. Within a few minutes
he stood before the doorway. He could see nothing inside.
Damn, he had forgotten to bring a torch! The water obstacle

had played so much on his mind, he had given no thought as to what conditions may be like within the tower.

Undeterred he entered into the darkness. He could hear a dripping sound and the place smelt dank. Looking up he could see dim light coming in through the smaller openings above. The soft glow allowed Stiles to make out the remains of a staircase rising out of the water and up around part of the interior wall, terminating in crumbled masonry. The dark water was just above his knees and the floor felt solid. It was slightly uneven though and Stiles had the impression of hard objects moving or cracking beneath his feet. A wave of profound isolation washed over him, as though the outside world of sunshine and flowers and birds was very distant. As though this place had been here, like this for hundreds of years, waiting.

He was wrenched out of his detachment by something brushing against his face - a soft touch, like the wing of a butterfly. Stiles turned sharply but could see nothing. Then something grasped his ankle.... and a shape emerged slowly from the water!

Stiles told me how to this day he couldn't properly describe the thing. 'It was like mud,' he said. 'Like a man, but made of mud!'

Dark and liquescent it rose up. His ankles, his arms, his waist, all were grasped in a cold, slimy, strong grip. Stiles cried out and fell to his knees, looking up. The thing bent towards him. There was no face, just a smooth, shiny, blackness, which moved forward as if to complete the embrace. Stiles passed out at that point.

He came round abruptly, coughing and spluttering. He was sprawled on the ground, on the trail, not far from the stone marker. The Major and Mrs Deverell stood over him looking concerned.

"There there old boy, have a swig of this!" The Major offered a flask and Stiles took a deep swig of the brandy. "What... where?"

"You are lucky we found you!" said Mrs Deverell. "After hearing you talking about Catfield Fen last night we thought we would come and have a look around the place. We found some of what looked like your equipment by that old stone marker and wondered if you had got into trouble. I said to the Major, well we can't just leave, can we, that poor young man may be in difficulties and -"

"Long story short," interrupted the Major, "after a bit of a search we came to that mere you were talking about and heard you splashing around and screaming. Well, I managed to get across and found you face down in the tower, covered in mud and coughing fit to burst. Close thing old boy, reckon you had slipped and fallen. You were close to drowning I'd say, even in a few feet of water!"

Stiles shivered and coughed some more.

"Did you see anything else?" he asked.

The Major exchanged a glance with his wife.

"Nothing, old chap, though there was one curious thing. Once I'd got you up and out I felt I was stepping on something. Anyway I reached down and pulled some old bones or something out of the water. Threw them away pretty sharp, I can tell you! Anyway, we dragged you out and here you are! Let's get you back to the Inn and cleaned up, shall we?"

◆

Stiles finished his sherry and looked up at me.

"So there we are Farnsworth, what do you make of that?"

"Well, on the face of it... you got caught up in the excitement of the chase, went into an old ruin, slipped, maybe banged your head, fell in the mud."

Stiles gave a grim smile. "That's what I'd like to believe too. And yet every night since that event I feel it. It wakes me. The soft touch of a butterfly wing against my face!"

"Are you sure Stiles, nasty shock like that is bound to have an effect on a chap?"

"Oh I'm sure... you see, he is letting me know. I escaped from him in the tower, but he wants me now. So he is coming for me."

"That was it, that was his story. With that, he shook my hand and off he went. " Farnsworth paused, looked up at us and took a puff of his pipe.

"Well it's a queer enough tale, " I said, "but it seems to me there's a perfectly reasonable explanation, as you said to Stiles yourself. "

Plympton and Longhurst nodded in agreement and, noting the time, rose from their chairs. As if on cue, Ashton appeared with our coats and scarves and soon our host was ushering us towards the front door, smiling and shaking hands with each of us in turn. We thanked him warmly for the company and dinner and were just making our exit into the crisp, night air, when Farnsworth raised a hand.

"Oh, there was just one other thing, " he mentioned sadly. "You see... Stiles was found dead in his bed just a few days ago. The sheets were covered in mud and, according to the doctor who attended, the cause of death was drowning."

With that he bade us goodnight and closed the door.

Remnants

THE FEN HOUND

Steve Bowden tucked his chin in and redoubled his efforts, legs pistoning on each side of the carbon bike frame. The long thin road lay ahead, straight as a die, bathed in the rosy glow of the setting sun.

Some thought it odd that Steve would be out cycling at this time of day. But, as he explained, the day of the big race was fast approaching and at this time the roads were quiet. Everyone was home from work and there were no lorries or agricultural traffic to contend with.

Steve was originally from Telford and had moved across to East Anglia after being poached by a bio-med company at Cambridge Science Park. Cycling had long been a passion, much easier here in the flat fens than the hills of his home county.

Another ten minutes and the sun was gone, the surrounding fields transforming from pink to grey to black. Steve paused to switch on his lights, front and back, then continued. Another ten miles should do it, a big circuit round this section of the Fens, then back to the car, home, shower, a bite to eat and bed.

Steve was nearing the end of the circuit, heading back to the pub where his car was parked, when he was bathed in the glow of headlights from behind. He heard the car - not the engine first of all, though that was loud enough, but the thump-thump-thump of a bass speaker. He glanced over his shoulder and moved slightly towards the grass verge. The verge was not wide and fell away sharply into the dark, still waters of the dyke below. The metallic blue car slowed slightly as it drew level with him and four white faces peered out. The passenger window wound down, the music even louder now, and Steve got a waft of cannabis.

"Wanker!" gestured the pale faced youth in the front passenger seat. "Bike wanker!"

Steve resolutely kept his gaze fixed ahead and stopped cycling, letting the bike glide. The car sped off, tail lights fading into the mist that was beginning to form. Steve let out a breath and resumed pedalling. The last thing he wanted out this way was trouble, there was no-one around for miles if he needed help.

He had just settled back into his rhythm when the low boom of techno music and the revving of an engine carried out of the mist. Full beam headlights speared into his eyes and Steve involuntarily threw an arm up across his face. The car screamed past, the bass pounding like a punch to the gut and something flew out of the window. There was the briefest glimpse of a spinning beer can, a breathless impression of the whirling ground and sky, then it all went dark.

Steve woke with a dull headache. He sat up slowly and took stock. His shoulder hurt, his knees and elbows were stinging, but there seemed to be nothing broken. Luckily the cycle helmet seemed to have taken the impact of the missile. A full beer can? Jesus....

The bike lay next to him on the soft, damp earth. He was lucky not to have gone into water; the road had turned away from the dyke a few hundred yards previous and was instead flanked by fields. It was pitch black now, the mist had thickened and Steve could not see more than a few feet in front of his face. By feel, he found his bike. A quick examination revealed a buckled front wheel and broken headlight. Shit, it was an expensive bike!

It then struck Steve that he may have a more pressing problem. He had no idea which way he was facing, or where he was. He seemed to be in a field, but could not see the road. There was no light, no welcome twinkle from a distant farmhouse, just the darkness and mist. Steve shakily got to his feet and pulled the mobile from his bum bag. The cracked screen gave a quick glow and then faded. Double shit.

With nothing else for it, Steve picked a direction and wheeling his broken bike alongside him, began a slow trudge into the gloom. Now he had stopped cycling, Steve quickly grew cold. The night air closed in, fingers of fog plucked at his clothing. His cycle boots sank slightly into the ground, which seemed to be getting muddier.

With a feeling of relief, Steve found a slight rise and went up it, onto the firmer ground of what felt like a track. Turning right he walked along it, shivering slightly. As he walked he couldn't help but turn his mind to all those old stories and folklore tales he had read when he learned he was moving out here. The phantom lights, the Fen witches and most all, of course, the tales of Black Shuck, the Fen Hound, whose appearance foretold death and doom.

Was it his imagination, or was there something moving alongside him, parallel to the track? It was difficult to see anything in this gloom. There, was that a shadow of movement? And that sound... could it be? The faint sound of a panting dog? Surely this was just a nightmare; he would wake up in a minute by the roadside or in a warm hospital bed. But even though he closed his eyes and shook his aching head, the noise continued.... very faint but still there.

Steve picked up his pace and was soon running at a slow jog. Suddenly to his horror he suddenly noticed that the track was gone. Had he wandered off it, or it had it just ended? The ground underfoot was definitely softer now; he was sinking up to his ankles in mud. The clinging mire slowed him down, though his breathing continued to be ragged. Above the sucking sounds from his feet he heard another noise - that panting again, closer now! Steve redoubled his efforts but ended up stepping into a deep pool and falling face first into water. Spluttering and coughing, he regained his feet. When he fell he had dropped the bike - where was it? He fumbled around briefly in the dark, but could find no trace of it. It had gone, somewhere into the water perhaps. Should he spend more time looking for it? It could be anywhere... and the ground was becoming more treacherous.

There was also the panting, close behind him now. It conjured all sorts of pictures in Steve's mind. He remembered descriptions of a calf-sized black hound with blazing eyes and slavering jaws. He began to move away from the sound. It moved with him.... to his right now, so Steve turned left. Then it seemed ahead of him and to the left... so Steve moved right. By some chance he was avoiding the deeper pools, though the ground continued to be marshy and sucking.

At that instant there was another sound, one that chilled Steve to the bone. A distant, haunting whistle.... two notes, long and low. There it was again, hard to determine which direction it came from. Now he heard the panting again, behind him! Steve stumbled on, panic setting in. Fortunately the ground was becoming a little firmer underfoot.

Up ahead he saw it - the dim glow of a light. How far away? Impossible to say. But wait! Steve stopped to catch his breath. It seemed to be moving, bobbing slightly. In the absence of any other sign of human life Steve moved towards the light.

With a lurch Steve found himself climbing a short slope and

he dropped to his hands and knees, thankful for the feel of even a simple dirt track under his outstretched palms. The light was ahead, definitely on the track. Was it leading him on? Was it one of the fabled will o wisps? If it was, at least he was back on firm ground. The panting had stopped too, was he out of Black Shuck's hunting ground?

Revitalised by fresh hope, Steve surged on. The bobbing light stayed at the same distance ahead. But then came the sound he dreaded, a sound that chilled him once more - the panting was back, close beside him! Steve began a desperate run now, but the panting stayed level with him, then actually drew ahead ! The bobbing light had stopped moving and Steve rushed towards it, feeling as though he was in a race for his life.

Suddenly Steve burst out of the fog and onto a tarmac road. He stopped to look around. Ahead a little, the track continued over on the other side of the road. At the junction, he could make out the figure of a man, carrying a walking staff topped by some kind of lantern. It was hard to make out any details; Steve got an impression of a large build and a pale face under a distinctive shaped hat. At the man's feet sat a white dog, not large, some kind of spaniel perhaps?

Steve stood unsure of what to do or where to go. As he did so the figure turned and, with the dog at his heels, took to the track, quickly fading into the mist. Steve stood alone on the tarmac, heart pounding. Turning around he saw the most beautiful sight.... the lights of a nearby buildings. He stepped along the road towards the glow, which soon resolved itself into a pub and some neighbouring houses. Steve found a street sign that said Raven's Drove and sat on it for a few minutes to compose himself. Then striding up to the pub door, he walked in.

The pub interior was warm and cosy, typical of its type. Three men sat at the bar, an elderly couple were at a table and a lone man sat in a corner. They all turned as Steve came in.

"By 'eck duck, what happened to you?" the large blonde lady behind the bar asked with what seemed like genuine concern.

"I.... that is I had a bit of an accident, I came off my bike."

They took in his mud-covered, torn clothes, the cut on his head, his shaky hands. One of the men stood up.

"Here, boy, sit yerself down, June, looks like this lad could do with a brandy!"

Within minutes, Steve found himself sat on a bar stool, nursing a large brandy, a blanket over his shoulders.

"Is there anyone you'd like to call?" The landlady indicated the phone at the end of the bar.

"No, thanks - although I guess I should call a cab to get back to my car, it's parked at The Oliver Twist at Guyhirn."

"Don't you worry about that, Peter here will drop you off, won't you duck?"

"No problem," said Peter, "I'm back off to Thorney in any case. Whenever you're ready son, no rush"

Steve stammered his thanks, feeling a rush of emotion at the locals' concern and help. As he sat he began looking around the bar and noticed a set of framed photographs hung on the wall opposite. They looked to be photos of village life and local people. One caught his eye and he got up to take a closer look. It was a black and white photo, taken out in a field, a large man in a distinctive shaped hat with a small white dog at his feet.

"That's them!" Steve pointed to the photo.

"That's who petal?" the landlady asked.

"Well when I was lost out in the field, I saw that man and his dog. They helped me back to the road. Who is he? I'd like to buy him a drink!"

No-one seemed inclined to answer and Steve caught, in the corner of his eye, the landlady mouthing the words 'head injury' to the other regulars. It was the elderly lady at the table who spoke.

"That there's Young Arthur and his dog, Lady. He were a big lad, Arthur, what we used call a bit simple. He wasn't treated well by his family, but he made his own way as best he could, bit of this, bit of that. Yes, a big lad, but a gentle giant, always ready to help. And he loved that dog, they were inseparable."

"Were? What do you mean *were*?" asked Steve.

"Well, they were seen going off up the old track one night and was never seen again. Folks presumed they were taken by the marsh, no trace was ever found of either of them. That photo, you see, was taken fifty years ago"

THE DUNWICH NIGHTMARE

Prologue

Light, so much light... and space! He stands, arms
outstretched, and circles slowly on the spot. No
walls. No locks. No pain. He squats, the white gown dragging in
the mud. Tilting his head back he sniffs a scent... clean, fresh. It
draws him on, away from the Place. He moves slowly at first
then, as the excitement of freedom fills his body, he begins to
run, to leap, to bound, sometimes upright, sometimes on all
fours.

His breath is ragged now, in great bursts, but he does not
slow or falter. Mud and mire cover him and he rejoices in its
feel. A light drizzle falls, he opens his mouth wide to taste it.
Every sensation fires him anew... he is free!

The land is crisscrossed with small creeks, icy cold. He crosses
them heedlessly, drawn on by the scent. Then, up and over a
small rise, he sees it, flat and grey in the dawn light. Shining,
whispering softly on the narrow strip of beach, the sea. To each
side it stretches, further than his eyes can see. He is drawn
towards it, crunching pebbles underfoot.

A distant memory flutters at the back of his mind. A place like
this, laughter, warm sun, people... and Other of course, he has
always been there. He goes to that space in his mind. He allows
the sights, sounds and smells to flood his being so that Other
may also experience them.

"I will be back for you, Other" he promises. A sound snaps
him back to the now. An animal, barking, snarling. He turns to
face a large dog, hackles raised, that cowers six feet from him.

"Rocky, come here! Rocky! Get back here, you bugger!"
A figure emerges through the light dawn mist.

"Sorry, mate," the man smiles and waves a lead towards the snarling dog. "He's friendly really. Don't worry, I'll put him back on the -"

The man stops as he takes in the figure in front of him. The tattered gown, spattered in filth, the eyes shining white in a mud-covered face. The figure draws itself up to its full height, looming over him. The man gives a cry and falls to his knees, arms crossed in front of his face as if to blot out the sight.

The man looks like one of the ones that hurt him! But now he is free! Now he can hurt them!

As the dog whimpers, wheels and then runs, the tall figure places a cold, bony hand on each side of the man's head, tilting his face up towards his own. The man's last sight is of insanely glowing eyes and jaws that keep opening... opening...

Chapter One

"And we can say, with confidence, that we believe the last person to see the victim alive was the murderer." Detective Sergeant Hinds winced inwardly as the words left his mouth. His first major press conference and he was making a real mess of it.

There were a few titters in the audience. His boss, Detective Inspector McCauliffe, took off his glasses and squeezed the bridge of his nose. Only the vivacious red-head Suzy, from The Ipswich Star, looked sympathetic.

"Any details on the victim?" asked a reporter at the back.

"Yes, we can confirm he is James Watling, age 62. A local

man, widower, living alone. His family have been informed, of
course. Mr Watling's body was discovered at approximately
7.45am after a local fishermen saw the deceased's dog, er," he
glanced at his notes, "Rocky, in an agitated state on the beach
near to Dunwich."

"Cause of death?" asked the same reporter, glancing at his
watch as he did so.

"Sorry, am I keeping you from something more important?"
Hinds felt like saying. Instead he said "we have yet to receive
the final autopsy report, but we can say that Mr Watling was
the victim of a savage attack. He received extensive injuries to
his head and upper body. Very extensive."

"Word is it looked like some kind of animal attack," Suzy
ventured. "Any truth in that, Sergeant?"

"Like I said, we are awaiting final lab reports before making
any further speculation. In the meantime we would, of course,
ask the public to be vigilant and also appeal for anyone with
any information to come forward. No matter how small or
unimportant you think it may be, it could help. People can get
in touch via their local station or direct to me here at Ipswich
HQ. Are there any other questions? Then thank you, ladies
and gents, we will let you know of any further developments."

The room quickly cleared, only Suzy lingered.

"Well, how did that feel, Marcus?" she asked.

"Scary! Far scarier than my first army patrol!" Hinds
admitted. "And almost as scary as a scolding from a West
Indian mother!"

Suzy laughed. "Don't worry, it gets better. At least you got
the name of the victim right! So you had a strict upbringing
then?"

"Yep, Mum and Dad were proper old school. Dad was a
stickler for discipline, I joined the army as a break! Mind you

I don't blame them, South London was no picnic back then,
especially for - "

"Hinds!" McCauliffe barked across the room. "My office,
now, look sharp!" Hinds shrugged. "A policeman's work is
never done," he grinned. "Catch you later, Suzy."

 Ozzy parked the car and got out, glancing around to see if
anyone was clocking him. Not likely, but it always paid to be
careful. He'd taken all the usual precautions while travelling
to and from the meet. It was a ball ache, but if you got
complacent, that's when they'd catch you. Ten years in the
animal activist scene had taught him that, if nothing else.

The meet had been at a dingy estate pub in Huntingdon, a
place Ozzy chose purposely because of its bad reputation.
Undercover types tended to stick out in places like that. His
contact, Chas, had finally come through. Chas worked at
Brampton Life Research, a longtime target for Ozzy's activist
group due to their continued use of animals in experiments.
In the old days, it had been all balaclavas and break-ins. These
days security had been beefed up so much you could barely
get near the place; more subtle methods had to be found.

The group had discovered that many minor support staff in
these labs felt uneasy about what went on there and could,
with a little charm or pressure, be persuaded to pass on
information. Chas had been persuaded - in any case, he was
agency staff and only had another couple of weeks left to run
on his contract, so what did he care?

Chas had handed over a couple of flash drives, explaining
he'd managed to nip into Admin on the sly and download a
wedge of files. What they were, he didn't know. Ozzy was
about to find out. Glancing round again, he unlocked the door
and went into his ground floor flat. A small place but he kept

it tidy and it served a purpose. A place to sleep, a place to eat and, as the large PC screen dominating the living room showed, a place he could research, communicate and co-ordinate - all through proxy servers, of course.

Once he had a cup of mint tea to hand, Ozzy fired up the PC and began to sort through the files. Day-to-day lab business was of little interest, though it might reveal details of companies who supplied the lab. Given the bad publicity over the last few years, these companies were not keen to make such connections known. It took some digging to find suppliers but, once they had been found, pressure could be applied. Even just the threat of making their involvement public may be enough to do the job.

There was nothing of use on the first drive but the second was more interesting. Ozzy almost missed it at first; it was only when he started working through sub-menus that he found a number of requests from a Dr Lange at a place called simply The Facility. These included questions on sourcing primate test subjects, details of local livestock suppliers and a request for the transfer of a Dr French to The Facility.

This was news indeed. BLR had been under pressure for to cancel its animal experimentation programs. Was this a sign that the work would be moving elsewhere, to a new secret lab? There was little further information in the files but Ozzy now had a couple of names to work with. He logged on to the dark web and began making enquiries.

Chapter Two

Mihai looked up from his work as a large, black car glided past. He watched as it swept round to The Facility entrance. A smartly dressed man in his fifties got out from the back and entered the sliding doors of reception. Mihai turned back to forking the hay and cleaning out the cows.

He was working in a covered cow shed that ran one length of The Facility compound. These days there might be up to a dozen cows; it was a bit like being on the farm back home in Romania. A bit, but not totally. There was the security here, for one, and the few odd things that went on. Still, the work was well paid and he was left to get on with it for the most part; taking care of the animals, general cleaning and maintenance, and occasionally driving into town for supplies or errands. East European workers were not high on the list for decent jobs and this was certainly better than the three weeks he'd spent picking sugar beet in cold fields. He even had a caravan, shared with another worker who'd just recently left; also an improvement in circumstances.

There was one part of the job he hated, though. For the past couple of weeks he had to lead a cow, every other day, up the ramp to the big door. The Airlock, everyone called it. It had only been installed last month, along with a new unit on the side of the main building. The big wheel in the centre reminded Mihai of one of those doorways on a submarine, though it was much larger. It must have been about three metres high, with a keypad on the side. It was Mihai's job to take a cow up the low ramp while one of the security staff opened the Airlock, lead the cow into the antechamber, remove the halter and then leave.

There was another door in the far wall of the antechamber, similar to the external one. Mihai had never seen that one open. As soon he was out, the external door was closed. He had no clue what happened to the cows but they never came back out. One time, he loitered by the Airlock hoping to hear something, but the security man shouted at him and ushered him away. Still, he shrugged to himself, this was the business of the people who ran the place, not his concern. He was getting paid and fed; let someone else worry.

Checking his fob watch, Hendry strode purposefully into the reception area. Outwardly, as always, he looked calm, sleek, immaculately suited. Inside, he was seething. He was not a man used to being on the carpet and this morning he had to suffer a fifteen minute dressing down from the Minister. He breezed straight past the security guard on the desk and strode down the corridor to Lange's office. He didn't bother to knock.

Dr Lange looked up from his laptop, totally unsurprised, it seemed, by Hendry's sudden appearance.

"Explain!" barked Hendry. "Is it true - was it one of ours?"

"We believe so, yes," Dr Lange quietly replied. He was a slight figure, grey haired, always in a white lab coat. He reminded Hendry of an absent-minded chemistry teacher he had had at prep school. But there was nothing absent-minded about Lange, his stare was intense and his mind was sharp.

"Subject D escaped late Tuesday night. We are still investigating exactly what happened, though it seems human error was to blame - one of the newer members of staff, who has since been... reprimanded. In any case, Subject D is now loose and, we believe, responsible for the murder."

"Local police?"

"We have had no contact with them as yet, though we are monitoring their investigation. In addition, we are making our own enquiries but, of course, our manpower is very limited. Beyond the medical staff, we have only a small security team and a couple of support workers. We don't have the capability to search miles of open marshland!"

"I'm aware of that, Lange, so I'm calling in a team to assist. They are a counter-terrorist unit currently on an exercise at Sizewell. They have high security clearance, though will obviously not be appraised of the full situation. As far as they are concerned, they will be hunting an escaped terrorist suspect. I'll put the Squad Leader directly in touch with you and I expect you to give him full cooperation. I will also need the full dossier on Subject D."

"Of course, of course. And our work in the meantime?"

"Continue as normal. I understand there have been new developments? You requisitioned a new secure unit recently?"

"Indeed. Subject E has exceeded expectations. We are very pleased with his progress. We have been experimenting with longer exposure times, you see? As a result, we are finding that the immediate alterations are more profound and they also continue to develop post-exposure."

"Good. You are to press on. Our friends in Europe will be keen to visit soon. They are hopeful for a major breakthrough prior to the new project going live."

Dr Lange removed his spectacles and gave a humourless smile. "A breakthrough? Oh yes, Hendry, I think we are very close to a breakthrough. You see, I believe we have made contact!"

"Contact with what, exactly?"

"Well, that is rather the question, Hendry. *That* is rather the question!" The doctor gave an unsettling laugh that followed Hendry as he walked back down the corridor to his waiting car.

The big light hurts, so he hides when it comes out. So many places to hide, burrows and old sheds... though he doesn't like those so much, they remind him of the room. When he rests, the beach memory comes back, clearer now; himself, a man and woman and Other, of course. Different, then. No pain or hunger. And the feeling of being at home, secure. Not in the room or in the Bad Place. Later, when the big light has gone, he wanders out again. He has no plan, though he knows he will return to help Other when he can. He sees some lights and moves towards them, curious.

Bill has just settled down with a mug of tea when the sound of the animals brings him to his feet. Pulling the curtain aside, he peers into the dark farmyard. *He really should get that security light fixed.*

He pulls on his coat, turns on the torch and tucks the shotgun under his arm, just in case. The cows are calling like mad; Bill has never heard the like. As he moves slowly across the gloomy farmyard, he sees one of the farm cats - its back arched into a high C, fur bristling. It yowls and hisses, moving backwards, looking up at...

Bill follows the cat's gaze as something moves out of the shadow and into view. A face, blood and mud streaked, pale as death in the torch beam. A man, tall, very tall, wearing some kind of hospital gown, the eyes have a fierce glow. Clean shaven, a tuft of wild hair on an otherwise bare scalp. The man walks forwards menacingly.

"Stop there, stop there, I've got a gun!" stutters Bill.

The man continues, grinning, spreading his arms wide. Bill fumbles with the shotgun, the torch beam flashing about in his shaky grip. The intruder swipes a hand, knocking the gun aside. It clatters away into the darkness.

In desperation, Bill grabs at the man's chest with his free hand, in a vain attempt to stop him. Bill stumbles, the gown ripping as he falls... and Bill sees what is underneath.

"Oh my God, sweet Lord have mercy! No! NO!"

Chapter Three

"Fancy a sandwich, Sarge?" PC Stammers presented a Tupperware box to Hinds.

"Stammers, how could you?" Hinds waved the offer away.

"Well, he won't mind, will he Sarge?" Stammers indicated the covered body that lay close by on the autopsy slab.

"Here we are, full notes, subject Watling J." Dr Barzetti came out of her office waving the folder. "Stammers, really!"

She looked disapprovingly at the young PC who, with a mouth full of sandwich, apologised. "Sorry, Doc, no time for breakfast this morning!"

"Never mind him," said Hinds, "what have you got, Doc?"

She led them over to the table, drawing back the sheet to reveal the naked, mutilated corpse. They both turned at the gagging sound as Stammers retched, dropping his lunchbox on the shiny floor.

"For fuck's sake, Stammers!" Hinds snapped. "Go get a mop and clean that up!" The ashen Stammers beat a hasty retreat. Hinds turned back to Barzetti. Shaking her head, she proceeded.

"Okay, well, as you can see, the deceased suffered multiple lacerations to the head, face and upper body. You will see how most of the face and throat have gone. Note the deep scratches to the chest and shoulders. Chunks of flesh missing from the arms... four fingers gone... and, if we turn him over... deep wounds to the back, deep enough to expose the spine in places."

"Cause of death, Doc?"

"If he didn't die of shock first then it was blood loss - the jugular was torn, so he would have bled out even without all the other wounds. Time of death is in the report."

"So, what did this? A dog?"

"Well, there are certainly a lot of bite wounds. But they don't match the profile of a dog. Neither do the claws. In fact, they both look human." Barzetti paused.

"But?" prompted Hinds. "There's a *but*, isn't there?"

"There is. The bite marks would indicate a maximum mouth opening larger than anything I've seen before. The claw marks indicate large hands. The strength would be considerable, though not beyond what we have seen from people on certain types of drug. Oh, and the missing parts are just that - missing. We presume they were swallowed."

"Right - so we are looking for some kind of cannibal drug addict? Or a bear on crystal meth?"

Barzetti hesitated again, looking strained.

"There's another *but*, isn't there?" Hinds asked.

"Yes. A big one, planet-sized. The bites left traces of saliva. We ran DNA tests, they came back as being... human-like."

"Human-like? What does that mean, surely saliva is either human or not?"

"Well, in this case, it's not. It's human saliva at its base, but there are biological anomalies that, frankly, had the lab guys scratching their heads."

"Contaminated samples? Some mistake? Or maybe the effects of drugs in the system?"

"I collected all the samples myself, had them all tested. You can never rule out a mistake, I suppose, but every procedure was followed. Nothing indicates contamination or the presence of any drug or known to us. Frankly, I'm at a loss."

"Okay, Doc. I'm open to speculation at this stage. We have

no reports of escaped prisoners or patients, no mispers , not so much as a single sighting of anything or anyone suspicious. I know it's a remote area up at Dunwich but that makes it even more likely that a stranger would stand out. "

"I'll try some more tests, maybe speak to a couple of colleagues to see if they have any thoughts." Barzetti handed him the folder.

"Thanks, Doc"

"Sarge, Sarge!" Stammers burst into the room.

"Could't find a mop, Stammers?" Hinds asked.

"It's not that, Sarge - it's Dunwich.... there's been another murder!"

It took Ozzy a couple of days but he got some encouraging leads. The best came from *Cosmic Bob*, a regular on one of the larger conspiracy forums. There was little information on Dr French, other than she was a Government neuro-scientist. However, Bob had interesting information on Dr Lange; he had worked at Porton Down, the UK military research centre. Bob had a special interest in this area and Ozzy asked him to dig further. More information came courtesy of Bob's cousin, who worked at Sizewell, the nuclear power station situated on the East Coast.

Piecing together everything sent over to him, along with what he gained from hacking local government files, Ozzy concluded that a new research centre had been built on an old farm site not far from Dunwich in Suffolk. Pulling up local maps of the area, he was able to identify the old farm but could find no trace of a facility of any kind. Local news articles had nothing but brief mentions of a proposed agricultural research centre in the area. Time to go take a look!

Suzy balanced her coffee, laptop case and a box of cupcakes as she pushed the office door with her shoulder.

"Morning all, sorry I'm late," she said as she placed the items on her desk.

"Hey Suzy!" Mike's head popped up over the partition. "Your boyfriend's been on the phone again!"

"What? Who?"

"You know, Crazy Bob, your conspiracy nut friend."

"Oh, you mean Cosmic," laughed Suzy. "What's he want this time, have aliens landed in Burstall?"

"Who knows? In any case, he's rung about eight times already this morning. I told him you'd ring back."

"Okay, thanks Mike. Might as well get it over with!"

Suzy checked the number on the Post-It note and dialled. The phone was answered before the second ring.

"Suzy! Listen, this is major. I mean mega. This is huuuge. There's this doctor with this secret lab, we thin they are using animals and - hang on, can anyone else hear this?"

"Hi Bob, how are you?" Suzy arched her eyebrows. "Now why don't you just slow down and tell me what this is about?"

"Better I meet you. Then you can see the evidence."

"Bob, you aren't wasting my time here, are you? I haven't forgotten all that stuff about the Mayor; I took some serious shit for that!"

"No, no, no, listen. Trust me, this is big. Just give me five minutes and then you'll see. I can be in town within the hour. I'll have all the info with me. You have to see this, Suzy, believe me!"

"Okay, okay," Suzy relented. "The Cricketers on Crown Street," she glanced at her watch, "I'll be there at noon. Five minutes, Bob, this better be worth it!"

Hinds swore as he stepped out of the car and into a deep puddle. The farmhouse was remote and run down, situated at the end of a long track on the edge of the Westleton Heath Nature Reserve. He ducked under the police tape and nodded to the Crime Scene Examiner.

"Alright Brian? So what have we got?"

"Morning, Marcus, mind where you step there - if you could follow the approach path, lovely." The balding, relentlessly cheerful Brian Marsden smiled and indicated the way.

"Deceased was discovered approximately 10.30 hours by the postman. He drove up in his van, saw the body lying in the yard here. Called it in, no one else has been on the scene as far as we know."

"Where's the postie now?" asked Hinds

"Uniform took a statement, we took his shoe prints and he's gone on his way. Here we go." He lifted a blue sheet.

Hinds cast an eye over the farmer's body. From a cursory glance, it looked to be in the same condition as the body on the slab.

"As you can see, looks very much like our friend on the beach."

"Anything else, Brian?"

"Yes, we have this. A torn part of it was found in the victim's hand, the rest was found just over there," Brian held up an exhibit bag. "It looks like a hospital gown."

"So, we can presume the killer was wearing this? Okay, where's the nearest hospital to here?"

"Ipswich, I'm guessing, or maybe up at Yarmouth. NHS at least. Of course there may be private hospitals or clinics around."

"That's great, I'll follow that up. What else?"

"Well, we've checked the house over. Looks like someone

has been through it; drawers are emptied, things pulled out."

"Valuables?" Hinds queried.

"There's not much but, what there is, is still there, it seems. There's cash in an envelope on the kitchen table, the deceased's wallet is still in his jacket hanging on the door. Could be some clothing missing, but nothing valuable."

"Not a robbery, then?"

"No, I'd say not, Marcus - just pure, bloody, murder."

"Brian, over here!" One of the forensics technicians waved to them from the far side of the yard. "We've found what may be footprints!"

The two men made their way over.

"Just here, the ground outside the yard is very soft and there was no rain last night."

Surely enough, a set of regularly shaped imprints led away from the farm, heading north.

"What's out there?" Hinds asked, glancing out at the misty heath.

"Nothing much, sir," replied the technician. "Heath, some woods, Dunwich forest, I believe. Then marshes and the sea. Apart from Dunwich itself, there's nothing until you get to Walberswick. Someone could disappear out there for days."

"Let's get the dogs in, then, Brian?" Hinds suggested.

"Wouldn't work," the young man interrupted. "Oh, begging your pardon, I've worked with K9. It's the terrain - water, mud, marsh, lots of creeks. Be like trying to follow a fart in a hurricane. Would be murder to find a trail out there sir."

"It will be murder if we don't, son." Hinds turned up the collar of his coat, sighed and turned back to the CSE.

"Okay thanks Brian, let me have the full report once it's typed up. I'll have a word with the Chief, we need to get some bodies down here for a ground search. I'll also see if we can get the whirlybird up, we'll have more chance of spotting someone from the air."

If there was a stereotype for a conspiracy theorist then Suzy guessed Bob was it. He was waiting nervously at a corner table in The Cricketers, nursing a cola and munching on a bag of crisps. Personal grooming certainly wasn't a priority with him and Suzy would have put money on the twenty-something still living with his mum. Having said that, he had come up with some good information in the past. He had a nose for ferreting things out, particularly via the web, that some people would rather stay hidden.

"Hi, Bob, how are you?" she slid into the seat opposite.

"Yes, good. Now, yes, listen. Look at this Suzy, look at this." He slid an A4 folder over the table. She opened it and began leafing through the papers inside.

"What am I looking at here, Bob?"

"A call went out a few days ago from this guy I know. He was looking for details on a Dr Lange. The name rang a bell, so I did some searching. He was involved in work at Porton Down about ten years back."

"That's the military research place, right? I thought that place had been shut down?"

"Oh no, it still goes on - animal experiments, bio-weapons, the lot. They keep it a lot quieter these days, especially since that poor airman died a couple of years ago. Anyway, this Lange was involved in some uber-secret project, but it was all closed down. Perhaps the place was drawing too much heat. So looks like they've relocated and gone on to bigger and better things."

"Alright Bob, so far so what. Where did they relocate to?"

"Just outside Dunwich."

Suzy felt the first trickle of something travel up her spine. "Dunwich… when?"

"Almost two years ago. Here, the guy sent me all the information he'd got. It's at an old, empty farm, well off the beaten track. Nothing overlooks it; it's surrounded by heath and marsh. I printed off some maps." He pulled more sheets from the folder.

"But that's not all. I have a cousin works at Sizewell. He did some digging for me. Seems this new research place is somehow linked into the Sizewell network."

"What does that mean?"

"It means that a small facility in an old farmhouse is tapping into a nuclear energy plant."

"What on earth for? What could need that much power?" Bob shrugged and took a swig of cola.

"Don't know. My cousin, Wayne, couldn't find out any more. But he just rang me this morning to tell me about the internal security team."

"Who are they?"

"Anti-terrorist unit. They are not there, if you know what I mean, but most major potential targets in the UK have them to hand. The Civil Nuclear Constabulary runs day-to-day security at power plants. But they can also call on these Special Forces units. Well, the Sizewell unit was running around this morning before haring off site according to Wayne."

"Interesting. So who would have the clout to put one of these units out in the field?"

"Got to be high level, military or intelligence I'd say. See, told you it was interesting! 'Cos you see, I was researching all this then I heard about the murder the other day. Coincidence? What do you think?"

"Have you been to the police with this, Bob?"

Bob snorted. "Have I fuck! What's the point, they are all run by the same people. Remember last time I went there, they just laughed at me but I was right about that killer, wasn't I? With the Masonic thing and all that?"

"Yes, Bob, you were. Alright, I tell you what - if I can take all this info, I'll start looking into it and see what more I can find out. In the meantime, you keep your ear to the ground and if you find anything, let me know. Here's my mobile number, you can call me on that - but just about this case, Bob. I'm not interested in lizard men or UFOs, got it?"

"Yes, yes, okay , yes, thanks, no UFOs okay!"

"Alright, take care Bob and I'll speak soon."

Suzy walked back to the office, folder tucked under her arm, in deep thought. As she got into the office, Mike was on his way out. "Keep your coat on," he said. "They've found another murder victim at Dunwich"

Chapter Four

Prior to the double murder, Suzy had heard very little of Dunwich. She was originally from the Midlands, moving over to Ipswich when she got the job at The Star a few years back. She knew it was once a large seaport in the Middle Ages, maybe the largest in the country at one time. She also knew that most of the town had been lost to erosion and the sea, until only a small village was left now. She recalled a local legend about how you could hear the old church bells tolling under the waves in a storm.

Stopping at off home to pack a small case and make a phone call, she took the A12 north out of Ipswich. Soon she was passing through picturesque villages, full of quaint

architecture. Suzy knew this area had lots of wildlife reserves
and was popular with tourists; even in late autumn,
everywhere seemed busy. As she got further up the coast the
villages thinned and the landscape became increasingly
sparse. Large, freshly-ploughed fields, edged with small
tracks leading off to middle-distance farmhouses.

North of Yoxford, Suzy took a right onto a B-road heading
for the coast. The surroundings immediately changed, the
road being raised slightly above the marshland that extended
away on all sides. Within a few minutes all signs of modern
life had disappeared. There was no other traffic, just the cry
and flutter of marsh birds.

Another five minutes or so brought her into a small village.
She followed a sign for Dunwich that took her down a narrow,
hedge-lined road leading out of the village.

After a few hundred yards, the hedges disappeared and the
countryside opened up into wild heathland. Fern and gorse,
with curious, stunted trees; the purple, green and yellow a
marked contrast to the dull, grey sky. As she drove on, the
trees thickened and tracks led off the main road at irregular
intervals to destinations unknown. Soon the trees grew over
the road giving Suzy the sensation of driving through a green
tunnel. Then, all of a sudden, she came out into daylight and
saw the first houses of Dunwich itself.

Some pleasant looking cottages bordered the road on her
left, then a sign indicated a turn to the beach. Suzy took the
turn, passed the ruins of an old abbey on the right and, almost
before she realised it, was quite literally at the end of the
road. Ahead was the entrance to a car park, beyond which she
could see the beach. Suzy swung left and pulled up outside
The Ship Inn, the bed and breakfast she had previously called
in order to book a room. She figured it might be worth staying

here for a couple of days in order to be right on top of the investigation.

Going through the door of The Ship Inn was like stepping into the past. The interior was low-beamed, full of nooks and crannies and bedecked with all types of marine relic, paintings and sea charts. A large fire roared in the inglenook and the place was busy with drinkers and diners. The friendly landlady showed her through to the accommodation at the back. There was nothing antique about her light and airy room; it was a modern extension the landlady explained. She told Suzy the village was a popular destination for bird watchers and tourists alike. "Everyone wants to see us before we drop off the edge of the map!" the landlady smiled.

Suzy freshened up, then wasted no time going back into the main bar, where she began talking to the regulars and locals. She almost wished she could report that they were surly, mistrustful and secretive, but she found everyone to be open and happy to talk to her. Of course they were all shocked about the murder - "and now a second one too!" But no-one seemed to have any ideas or clues as to who the killer may be.

Suzy decided to take a look at the first murder scene. She crossed over the road and up to the beach car park, noticing an unoccupied police car. She walked across to the beach itself, somewhat surprised at how small it was. The tide was in, hissing at the shingle. There were a couple of boats and an old winch mechanism. To left and right the beach stretched into the distance, bordered by the grey sea on one side and low, crumbling cliffs on the other.

To the south she could make out the looming shape of a large, white dome - the Sizewell power plant. To the north, the coastline disappeared into the haze. She heard voices in the car park behind her and turned. To her delight, she saw Hinds pointing to a map and speaking to a couple of uniformed officers. He folded the map as the officers walked away, then he turned and saw her.

"A man who can fold a map, now there's a rare skill!" she smiled.

"Just one of my many talents, "he chuckled. "What brings you here?"

"I heard about the second murder, thought I'd come up and look around. What can you tell me?" She flipped open her notebook.

"The Chief is holding a press conference at HQ in an hour, but, as it's you. Victim was a farmer, William Driscoll. His farm is just a couple of miles over there." He pointed back towards the village.

"Same MO from the looks of it, savage wounds, no robbery. Seems like a random attack, victim had no enemies, he lived alone. Looks like he was just in the wrong place at the wrong time."

Suzy looked up from her notes. "Any suspects or ideas yet?"

"Best guess - we could be looking for an escaped psychiatric patient. We found a hospital gown and footprints leading off into the marsh. We have a couple of teams out there now and are hoping to get the chopper up before the day is out - hey, how about that for timing!"

The thrum of helicopter blades swelled then broke, as the police chopper came in along the coast, parallel to the beach. It passed them before making a ninety degree turn inland.

"Locals are all on alert; we think the suspect is on foot. This is not an area we can easily cordon off but there's not many places to go. We hope if the killer shows his face again we can nab him."

"Listen, about the hospital gown, I have some information that might help."

"Okay, I'm all ears."

Suzy briefly ran through the conversation she had with Bob, leaving out some of his wilder ideas. She flicked back a few pages and gave Hinds the details of the farm.

"Alright, that's great. I'll make some enquiries and see what we can find out. So are you staying locally then? "

"Yep, just over at the Ship Inn. The rooms are really nice there. You could have a look at mine if you like?"

Hinds grinned. "Thanks, Suze, but I've got to supervise the search teams. Maybe some other time?"

Suzi pouted "Is it 'cos I is ginger?"

"No, it isn't and you are a stunning redhead. It's just that well, since Nicole died in the accident... it's one of the reasons I transferred out here from Streatham. New start and all that. One step at time, you know?"

"Sure, I understand, but I will take you up on that offer. Oh, looks like someone wants you."

Hinds turned to see uniform rushing over to him "You see, like I said.... my work is never done! Laters!"

Mihai knew he should have headed straight back to The Facility after getting the supplies. But he had finished his duties for the day and the only thing to do back there was play solitaire in his caravan. So instead, he decided to treat himself to a meal at The Kings Head in Yoxford. Even better, he had made a friend! It wasn't often he got to talk to anyone new, so Mihai was pleased when the man started to chat with him at the bar, he had even bought him a drink or two. What Mihai didn't know is that the man, who had been sitting very patiently near the entrance to The Facility for many hours, had followed him as he carried out his shopping duties.

Mihai never the noticed the same man trailing him back to The Facility either. But then Ozzy was something of a self-taught expert in surveillance, having had many years practice from his activities. Ozzy drove on as Mihai's van turned into a narrow track off one the back lanes. He gave it a few minutes, before swinging the car around and parking up amongst some bushes. He walked to the top of the track and, sticking close to the trees and shrubs, moved down it. After about twenty feet, he came to a wooden five bar gate. There didn't seem to be any security but, after careful examination, he noticed a contact sensor on the gatepost. Opening the gate would trigger a signal further down the line.

Looking around and seeing nothing or no one, Ozzy climbed over the gate, being careful not to rattle it. Sticking to the edge of the track, he continued another twenty yards on, where the track curved to the right. Peering round the bend, Ozzy saw a large, metal double gate ahead, set into a fifteen foot high, weldmesh fence. There was no visible lock on the gate, but there was a card swipe and an intercom. Ozzy smiled and his fingers closed around the ID card he had lifted from Mihai's jacket earlier in the pub.

He decided to wait until later that night before attempting to gain entrance. A noise interrupted his thoughts - the crunch of tyres on the track! Crouching out of sight in the dark undergrowth, he watched as a light blue Volvo drove up to the gates.

A tall, smartly dressed black man in his late thirties got out of the car and walked up to the intercom. Ozzy could tell he was Old Bill, it was written all over him. The man spoke into the intercom for then waited. There was a loud buzz and click and gates swung inward. The man returned to his car and drove through, the gates slowly swinging shut behind him.

Ozzy trotted back to his car and moved it further off road, finding a place where he could watch the junction of track and road without being visible himself. He settled in and waited.

Chapter Five

He sleeps, wrapped in an old overcoat covered over with ferns, in a hollow in the ground. He dream-speaks with Other, sharing the sensations of his new-found freedom. What he sees, hears, tastes, feels, Other feels too. "Soon I will return for you," he promises.

In the dream he can hear his heart, a rhythmic thump. Then the thump becomes louder, enveloping him. He suddenly wakes, realising the thumping sound is not in him, but around him. He moves carefully to look out into the bright light. The sound is louder and he sees its source. There, up in the sky, a thing hovers. It moves slowly, almost directly over him at one point. His lips draw back in a snarl and he stretches his claw-tipped fingers. He senses it is them, come to take him back. He withdraws deeper into cover and soon the noise fades. He realises he is breathing hard. He will move once it is dark again. Move and feed. He needs all his strength if he is to help Other.

At the farmhouse Hinds was wrapping up with the search teams. Nothing had been found in the time available, the tracks had petered out once they reached the marshland. The helicopter crew radioed in that they had spotted nothing, but were preparing to do a sweep after sunset using night search technology. Hinds glanced at his watch and his belly growled. It was gone five and he'd not eaten since breakfast. He pulled out the details of The Facility that Suzy had given him and figured he had to time to grab a bite to eat before calling in there on the way back to Ipswich.

About an hour later, with a burger and chips sitting heavily in his stomach, Hinds was on the small back road that led to The Facility. He missed the entrance on first pass but swung back, and, after opening a five bar gate, drove down the track to a perimeter fence and security gate. Getting out of the car, he stretched and looked round. The track was bordered on both sides by trees and thick undergrowth; nothing could be seen of the surrounding countryside. He walked up to the gates and pressed the buzzer.

"Yes?" came a slightly accented voice.

"I'm Detective Sergeant Hinds, Suffolk Police. I'm investigating two local murders, I'd like to speak to whoever is in charge."

"Please wait," the disembodied voice replied. A couple of minutes passed, then, with a buzz and a click the gates swung open. Hinds got back into his car and drove through.

The track twisted and turned or another half mile or so before terminating in an old farmyard. To his left, Hinds saw a cattle shed and animal pens. There were half a dozen white caravans, an old farmhouse and a couple of outbuildings. A figure in security uniform waved a torch at him, indicating he should follow.

The driveway continued round to a car park area, where Hinds was surprised to see a small complex of modern buildings. Hinds parked and got out the car, the security guard saying "This way please, follow me."

Hinds placed the accent as maybe Polish, certainly East European. The buildings were connected by short corridors, a central building and three outlying ones, forming a triangle.

Hinds clocked the CCTV cameras. He also noticed a ramp on one of the outbuildings. It lead up to a door that would not have looked out of place in a high security bank vault.

"What's in there, then?" he asked the guard. There was no reply. Hinds shrugged and followed on. The guard swiped a card at the main entrance and led Hinds into a reception area. Another guard sat behind a desk. He nodded to the first guard and looked Hinds up and down.

"Wait here, please, "again, the accent.

After a short wait, a slight figure in a white lab coat entered reception. Male, late sixties, wireless specs, close cropped silver-grey hair. Ignoring the lurking security guards, he strode directly up to Hinds.

"DS Hinds? I am Dr Lange, Chief Medical Officer," he extended a hand, which Hinds shook firmly.

"Please, let's talk in my office."

Hinds followed the Doctor along a short corridor and into a sparse office. Hinds noticed no personal effects at all; there were no photos, certificates, no paintings on the wall. Lange indicated a chair and sat himself behind the desk.

"So, what can we do for our local police service?"

Hinds removed the evidence bag from his case and, showed Dr Lange the remains of the hospital gown.

"Do you recognise this item of clothing, doctor?"

"It would appear to be a standard hospital gown, no?"

"Indeed. The thing is, doctor, we know of no other hospital or medical facility within forty miles of where this gown was found, other than this one."

"And how did you come to know about this one?" Lange asked.

"I received information from local sources." Hinds countered.

"I see. Well, I am afraid to say you have had a wasted journey, Sergeant. This is a Government research facility; we have no patients here, only clinical trial volunteers, all of whom are present and accounted for. As you can see, we have full security measures in place. I'm sure you understand that such facilities as ours have often been targets of extremist groups. Our best security is that no-one knows we are here, or at least that is what we believed. So it disturbs me, Sergeant, that you received 'local knowledge' about us!"

"Oh, you know how it is, it's difficult to keep anything quiet in these small rural communities. I mean it must have taken some manpower to put all this together?"

"Not so much as you might think, Sergeant. These days wonders can be done with pre-fabricated units, even for specialist centres, such as ours."

"Specialist? May I ask what you specialise in here, Doctor?" Lange steepled his fingers, considered the question for a moment, then nodded.

"We specialise in what you might call fringe science. We push the boundaries of what is considered possible."

"To what ends, sir?"

"Why, that is simple - our aims are to encourage and advance the evolution of the human race."

"So, it's genetics, DNA?"

Lange laughed. "Genetics? We are far beyond that, Sergeant. You see, mankind has always posited the existence of higher intelligences than its own. Every culture has its creation myth; every culture has its methods of contacting their higher powers. Call it religion, mythology, superstition. But here, we have turned it into science!"

"What exactly are we talking about here? The paranormal? Aliens?"

Lange laughed again. "Little green men? Hardly. But we have made contact, Sergeant! Oh yes; we have made contact with something. Come, I will show you!"

Lange led the way out of the office and down the corridor into one of the adjoining buildings, which had the appearance and smell of a medical unit. There were several rooms off the central hub, many of them with an observation window in the door. Two white coated staff moved from door to door making notes on clip boards. At the far side of the hub was a large security door. Lange swiped his card and the door opened with a slight hiss. Hinds found himself in a large room. The wall opposite had a single, large window in it, with a heavy door to one side. In front of it was a bank of computer equipment and two swivel chairs. Lange pointed to the glass.

"Look, in there, Sergeant. Our pride and joy!"

Hinds moved up to the glass and looked through. The room beyond appeared to be lined with a metallic material. The room was empty except for a large, upright, circular device. It stood about ten feet high and the circumference was comprised of a narrow tube. At intervals around the tube were boxes about two feet square, each with three lights. A large snake of cables ran from the bottom of the structure to a duct in the wall.

Lange flicked a sequence of switches on the console. A deep, low hum filled the room. The lights on the structure began to flicker in regular sequence. A faint glow pulsed and intensified around the edge of the circle until the chamber was filled with a shifting iridescence that Hinds found hard to place on the spectrum .

"Now," said Lange, "tell me what you see!"

Hinds peered closely. He suddenly realised he could no longer see the wall through the other side of the device. The middle of the circle was black. It wasn't that it was dark, it was that there was a total absence of light.

"Looks like a black hole," he ventured.

"Very good, Sergeant! In fact that is almost what it is. And, perhaps like a black hole, it goes somewhere!"

"To where? Doesn't anything that goes into a black hole get crushed?"

"Ah yes it does - and we did have some problems initially. But, you see, a black hole is part of our own universe. What we have here is a gateway to another place entirely. A gateway that can be used, Sergeant, used to go to that other place and then return!"

"You put people through this?"

"No, not at first. We used various types of organism, then animals, working up to primates. It was a some time before we felt confident enough to use a human subject."

"Human? And did they come back?"

"Indeed, they did - but this is the interesting part. You see, they came back... changed. You might say they brought something of the other place back with them. They also exhibit special qualities. These were not always evident at first. There was often an obvious minor physical change, but we also began to see other developments - precognition, telepathy, even more profound bio-physical changes. This is what I mean by evolution, Sergeant. This is how we jump start the next stage of human development. Not by splicing genes in test tubes but by interacting with those intelligences from beyond!"

"Are you telling me there are things living out there?"

"Remember what I said earlier about myths and magic? You see, for generations occultists have searched for these secrets. Using crude methods such as human sacrifice, rituals, drug use, they attempted to *break through*, as it were. All largely useless, of course, though certain of them could be effective in very precise circumstances. Here, all we need do is throw a switch and we have access! But this is only the start. What you see here is a prototype. It takes huge amounts of energy to operate and is still prone to problems. Our work here is forming the base for something greater. Even as we speak, below the French Alps a facility is being built that will make this look like a child's toy! Once operational, we can only guess at the knowledge it will bring forth!"

Hinds swayed slightly as he struggled to take all this in.

"And the people you sent through?"

"They are still here. Come! See!"

Lange shut down the device and led Hinds back into the central, indicating the various doors.

"See for yourself."

Hinds looked into a couple of the rooms. They looked like standard hospital rooms, each with a figure lying in a bed.

"You see, all perfectly fine," Lange smiled. Just then a small voice spoke behind Hinds.

"Will mummy be here soon?"

He turned to see a young girl of around five or six looking up at him. She held a small, raggedy doll in one hand. A mop of brown, curly hair framed her round face; she stared at him with green eyes. There was a slight hint of accent in her voice.

"Hello there. What's your name?" he smiled and bent towards her.

"My name is Karina and I'm five and a half. Will mummy be here soon?"

The girl lifted her other hand and Hinds automatically extended his arm to hold it. Except it didn't feel like a hand. When he glanced down it didn't look like one, either. It was white, glistening and white, contrasting sharply with his dark skin. Instead of fingers there were four long flaccid, tapering digits, with a vague suggestion of the boneless about them. The tapers quivered, like underwater fronds or, Hinds thought, like the tentacles of a squid. And they felt cold... icy cold. With a start Hinds drew back.

"I'm sorry, Marcus, did I frighten you? "the girl asked.

One of the staff members hurried over, a dark haired woman.

"Ah, Karina, there you are. Come on, now, no wandering around. You know it's time for bed!"

" Sorry, Dr French. Will mummy be here soon?" The girl turned and allowed herself to be led off to her room.

Hinds was in a cold sweat. "What the hell was that? Some sort of deformity?"

"Deformity? Deformity? I show you an advance in the human condition and you call it a deformity! Your attitude is typical, Sergeant, I'm afraid to say. These people are not deformed!" Lange's voice was raising in pitch. "They are the next stage of the human race! They are the vanguard! The standard bearers of what is to come!"

The doctor gestured around, his eyes growing wild. Hinds could hear movement in the surrounding rooms, then the murmurings of the occupants. As Lange continued the voices increased in volume.

"These people are the future! They will shape the human race and lead it to a new destiny! They will endure and all your old human values and institutions will crumble! Those who refuse to be absorbed will perish in the filth of their own ignorance! This is the new millennium!"

The voices from the rooms were howling now, at fever pitch, and Hinds staggered back along the corridor followed by

Lange's laughter. He fled out of the building and back to his car. Breathlessly, he fumbled for his keys, then tore back down the track to the main road and sanity.

Ozzy was snapped out his daydream by a flash of lights at the track. He sidled out his car to get a better view, concealing himself in the dark undergrowth. It was the Volvo again. He watched as the man opened the farm gate then drove through and back up onto the road, leaving the gate open. At the junction, he watched as the man got out of the car and retched onto the verge. After a few minutes the man took some deep breaths, and is hands over his face, before getting back in the car and driving off at speed.

Ozzy wondered what could have caused that. Glancing at his watch, he saw it was half nine. People were still obviously up and about in The Facility at the moment; he'd go in at about four in the morning. Moving back to his car, he set the alarm on his watch and settled in for some shuteye.

Suzy walks slowly across the deserted beach. The sea is calm and quiet, just a regular ripple disturbing the shiny surface. The large, full moon gives everything the colour of bone. To left and right the shoreline fades into the distance. Looking north, she thinks she glimpses the outline of a figure atop the low cliff. For a moment it stands, silhouetted against the sky. When she looks back to check, it is gone. But now there is a figure on the beach, hundreds of yards away. It is indistinct, little more than a shape, but seems twisted, distorted. She can make out no features but has the sense it is watching her.

Her heart is pounding now, louder than the surf. She turns southward and begins a hurried walk away from the figure, shingle grating underfoot. After about twenty paces she glances

over her shoulder. The figure is nearer. It moves with a curious
shambling gait, awkward, broken, rising and falling. She turns
and begins to run, her progress slow on the shifting surface,
almost as if she were running on the spot. She hears it now,
ragged breathing, the crunch of its progress, drawing nearer.

Suzy is at full sprint. Ahead the pale strand leads on; there is
no hiding place, the vague shape of the power plant looms in
the distance. She risks another look over her shoulder - the
thing is less than ten feet behind her! Impossibly tall, a pale,
grinning face, black rags streaming out behind it. She falls
awkwardly, knees grazing on the sharp stones. The thing
reaches out bony hands, clawed, curved bony hands that reach
for her, reach for her...

Suzy was woken by the buzzing of her phone. With a start
she sat up in the bed. Reaching for the phone, she checked the
caller and pressed answer.

"Bob - what on earth are you doing, it's three in the
morning!"

"Yes, oh, yep, er, hi Suzy it's Bob. Listen I got some more
information. Thought you should hear it."

"Okay Bob, what is it?" She swivelled round cradling the
phone and reached for her notepad and pen.

"Okay yep, well I've been doing some more research on this
Dr Lange. I had to go back some way and pull some very deep
records, but what I found was that he came over to the UK in
1945 with his father. You ever heard of Operation Paperclip?"

"No, Bob, I don't think I have."

"It was a program run by the OSS - US Intelligence - after the
war. They brought over a thousand former Nazi scientists
and engineers to the USA. Some of those, like Werner Braun,
formed the base of the whole NASA Apollo programme. The

Soviets had a similar thing going on, and so did we. SIS was working mostly against the Soviets, but they did also recruit former Nazis to "the cause". One area of interest to them was the occult. It was something the Americans and Soviets had little interest in, but the Brits did, we always have. After all Dr Dee was the first 007! And it was Ian Fleming who suggested using Crowley, there was the whole Rudolf Hess thing, Dion Fortune was involved in that. It was-"

"Bob, Bob - Dr Lange?" interrupted Suzy.

"Ah yep, okay, well, the Germans had this thing called *The Ahnenerbe*. It was founded by Himmler and carried out research, expeditions and experiments into all aspects of occultism. Hitler and Himmler were fascinated by the occult and its modern day potential. Dr Lange's father was an Obersturmbannfuhrer in the SS and headed a research team at Schloss Oberkirchberg near Ulm. They were researching methods of contacting what they called "higher intelligences"; their methods, by all accounts, involved rituals and human sacrifice. They scoured Europe for hidden lore and old books; it is believed they had one of few full copies of the *Necronomicon!*"

"The Necro-what? What the hell is that?"

"Hell indeed - think of it as a key to opening the gate to those other higher intelligences."

"Bob, this is sounding like some mad fantasy. Is this for real?"

"Oh, it is very real! There's even film footage of the rituals and experiments. One thing about the Nazis, they were meticulous in keeping records. Anyway, point is, that after the war, Obersturmbannfuhrer Lange and his wife and son were spirited away to the UK. It's not clear exactly where he went and what he did, but there are death certificates, 1953 for him, 1958 for his wife. Lange Junior had a private education and his name then pops up, like I said before, at Porton Down and one or two other places. I presume he is carrying on his father's work."

"So let me get this straight, Bob. You are telling me that the guy running this facility near Dunwich, is involved in Nazi black magic experiments, human sacrifice and summoning demons?"

"No, not demons. Forget all that. This is about establishing contact with entities, beings from another place. Another dimension, perhaps. The spaces in-between. It's real, Suzy; these people don't waste their time on fairytales."

"Okay, Bob, so what now?"

"Well, like I said, I thought this was big but this knocks it out of the ballpark. Of course, you realise you can't print any of this?"

"Why not?"

"Durr, Suzy, it was all set up by SIS - that's now MI6! It's Government run. You know what happens to people who leak that stuff, they end up being suicided!"

"Oh, come on Bob, really? "

"Suzy, listen, I could show you cases and things. Look, just be careful who you tell what to, okay? Trust no one! I'm gonna do some more research. I thought I might come up there and-"

"No, no, Bob, you stay where you are. Now listen to me, this is all very interesting but, according to the police, what we have on our hands here is probably an escaped lunatic. He is still at large and wandering around, I want you to stay down there in Chelmsford where I know you are safe, okay?"

"Yep, okay yep ,well okay."

"Alright... well thanks for the call, Bob, I'm going now, I'll speak to you soon. Goodnight."

"Night, Suzy."

As she went to switch off her phone Suzy noticed a text flashing. It was from Marcus. *CALL ME ASAP*. Must have come in after she went to bed. Well, she would ring him in the morning.

Chapter Six

The chopper banked low and began another search pattern over the heath and marshland below. The infrared worked a treat here. Unlike most of the country there was no light pollution across the search area. A few lights at Dunwich, then nothing until much further up the coast or inland. On the third sweep, the observer called to the pilot, "I think we have something!"

The pilot took the chopper down to fifty feet and hovered over the indicated area. "There, look!" They could see a shape on the screen, moving fast across the black terrain. It paused and stopped, as though it were looking up at them.

"What size is that, doesn't look very big?"

"Yep, the heat signature doesn't look human. Probably a seal or a deer or something? Okay, let's continue north."

The horrible noise goes and he moves once more. His own night vision reveals small furry creatures around; sometimes they have to do as food. He is drawn southwards, back towards Other. But them are there, patrolling the narrow lanes with painful shiny-lights. He can wait. He draws back into the marshland... back towards the sea.

Ozzy made his final preparations and headed up the farm

track. The wooden gate had been closed at some point, but all was quiet and empty. Reaching the metal gates, he took a deep breath, then swiped the stolen card. With a click the gate opened...the card worked! He stole inside the perimeter and began a slow, careful jog along the edge of the track. Presently he came to a farmyard. Skirting the building he followed the driveway, until he came to the complex at the back of the site. The whole place appeared quiet. Using a digital camera, he began taking snaps, making sure the flash was switched off.

He moved towards the main entrance of the building. Through the glass doors he could see a dimly lit reception area, unmanned. Swiping the card again, the doors hissed open and he entered the building. Through the reception area, he had a choice of three directions. He chose left. The only illumination was from dim, recessed lights in the ceiling. He tried door handles as he went along. They all opened onto storerooms and cleaning cupboards. The corridor then opened out into a larger room which looked like an office area, containing a number of desks and PC terminals. There were three doors .

Opening one of the doors, Ozzy found himself in a dark room. Flicking on his torch he saw it was full of bookshelves, loaded with boxes, old books and stacks of papers. He moved to the nearest shelf, glancing at a ribbon-bound dossier with a green cover. The cover caught his eye, German writing, with an eagle and a swastika stamp! He took some more pictures, then moved to a filing cabinet in the corner. Opening a draw at random, he rifled through and pulled out a file.

It was full of letters, in an East European language. He worked out it must be Romanian, judging from the address at the top of one of the letters. Clipped to the letter were passport style photos of children. He stuffed a handful of letters into his backpack, shut the drawer and left the room.

Returning to the office, Ozzy tried another door. This led into a laboratory. Electrical equipment was scatted on bench surfaces; a large white board was covered in indecipherable squiggles and formulae. An opening on the other side of the room led to a break area. Ozzy returned to the main office and tried the third door. This opened up onto another corridor, which led into what looked like a medical area. Doors, some with observation windows, lined the walls. Ozzy risked a quick peek into a couple of them, but could see nothing more than a vague form in a bed.

One door had a card reader. Ozzy tried swiping the card a few times, but nothing happened. So he turned his attention to another windowless door. This led into a security room, a chair and desk above which a bank of monitors cast a pale glow. He was about to leave when a movement on one of the screens caught his eye. He moved forward and sat at the chair.

Most of the monitors showed external views of The Facility. One showed the reception area. But on one, something was moving. The picture was monochrome, slightly grainy. Ozzy was having a problem understanding just what he was looking at. Something large and grey moved across the screen. Then it turned and Ozzy jumped as a face looked directly at him, as though it knew he was there.

The face was of a young man, but there was something odd about it, something about the proportions. It was clean shaven apart from a wild tuft of hair and the eyes seemed curiously luminous. The gaze of the face held his own, he found himself moving closer to the screen. Then the face smiled and the jaws opened, far wider than jaws ever should, revealing sharp, pointed teeth. Ozzy watched in rapt horror, then flinched as the thing made a sudden lunge forward, jaws snapping shut. But that wasn't the worst part. Having lunged forward, the face now moved back... way back... and Ozzy saw what it was attached too.

Words like *spider, crab, octopus* flashed through his brain in a futile attempt to attach some meaning or coherence to what his eyes were seeing. But no meaning came. He had a disjointed impression of a flabby bulk supporting a long, thick neck atop which the face waved and turned. A vague sense of eyes and mouths where none should be. There was a jumble of tentacles, of many-jointed legs, undulating horribly. From the size of the face, dear God, the thing must be huge!

With a strangled cry, Ozzy fell back... and that's when all the lights came on. Two security guards entered, along with an older, grey haired man in a smart dressing gown.

"Well now,what do we have here? A visitor for one of our inmates, perhaps?" The older man gestured to the guards. "Search him!"

Ozzy found himself dragged out and into a smaller hospital-like room. His brain was still struggling to make sense of the vision on the monitors, his body paralysed by shock. Before he knew it , he was being strapped onto a trolley.

The feeling of restraint spurred Ozzy back into action. He began kicking and struggle, shouting wildly to be let free. The older man turned away, then came back into view holding a syringe. "First, we shall give you this small sedative....then I shall return later for a conversation."

Ozzy flinched as the needle pushed into his arm, then all went dark.

It was some hours later when Ozzy came round. He felt confused and groggy. He remained strapped to the gurney.

"What.. where am I?"

"You are still in The Facility, young man. I am Dr Lange. Now, we need to establish who you are and why you are here. We have some food and drink for you, then we shall ask you some questions. There will be another injection, I'm afraid, in order to ensure the veracity of your answers."

A guard brought in a tray with some food, but Ozzy had no appetite. His brain was still struggling with what he seen on the monitor. He declined the food and attempted another futile struggle against the restraints. The doctor prepared another syringe... and the questioning began.

It was late afternoon when Ozzy recovered his wits again. The last few hours were a blur in his mind; he remembered little more than the soft, low voice of the doctor. He was still restrained, unable to move from the trolley. A security guard opened the door and the doctor entered with another guard in tow.

"Well now, young man, we have checked your information and made our own enquiries. It seems you are acting alone and no one knows you are here. As that is the case, I have an important task for you. It is a privilege, in fact! "

"What do you mean, what are you talking about?" Ozzy struggled again to no avail.

"Well, you see, we have yet to determine how Subject E will react to normal people. We know something of his dietary preferences, of course, but little else. Direct communication has so far proved problematical but I'm sure he has much to tell us! Subject E is our greatest success to date. He is the one who has changed the most since he came back. A glorious specimen, don't you think? So, young man, we will introduce you to Subject E and we shall see what happens! I shan't be far away, I shall be monitoring via the camera and microphones. To be honest, I'm not sure if he will eat you, mate with you or talk with you. Perhaps all three! Let's find out!"

He signalled to the guards, who wheeled the trolley out and back towards the reception area. Ozzy writhed, he began screaming, but his pleas went unanswered. Within minutes they were outside the building, the gurney being pushed up a ramp towards the Airlock. Ozzy was babbling by now, tears streaming down his face. The guards remained impassive as they opened the large door and wheeled him into the antechamber.

His last glimpse of the outside world was of the dying rays of the setting sun through the closing gap of the outer door. There was a short pause, then a loud hiss as the inner door began to slowly swing open....

Mihai had finished work for the day and was eating in his caravan when a noise from outside caught his attention. Pulling the curtain aside a little, he saw two guards pushing a trolley round the side of the building towards the Airlock. Curious, he slipped quietly out of the caravan. Shivering in the twilight air, he crept around the other caravans and positioned himself in view of the ramp. He could see the figures clearly now. The man on the trolley was thrashing and crying, but the guards ignored him.

There was a bulkhead light above the Airlock. As the gurney was pushed up the ramp, the man turned and Mihai got a glimpse of his face - it was his friend from the pub! What was going on? The screams faded as the two guards came back out of the chamber and closed the outer door.

Mihai's shivering intensified, though not because of the

cold. My God, did that man have his missing security card? He had already got into trouble earlier, telling the guard he forgot to take the swipe card out with him. What would happen now? His co-worker had recently left suddenly, to return home, Mihai had been told. Now he wondered. He knew his friend had made some mistake too. He made a snap decision. Creeping back into the caravan, he gathered his few belongings, threw on some clothes and fled down the track into the darkening gloom.

Hinds groped blindly for his mobile, eyes squinting against the bright, morning glare. He'd only had one whisky when he got home last night , but felt very hung-over. His sleep had been interrupted by vague, unsettling dreams. His head still ached at the thought of that weird glow from Lange's device.

He found the phone and answered. It was Suzy. They both spoke at the same time, eager to share last night's experiences. Eventually they agreed to meet up later that day to swap notes.

As Marcus showered he thought back to what had happened at The Facility. Maybe his memory had played tricks, after all what had he actually seen - a poor young girl with a deformed hand, an eccentric scientist, some funny lights? The rest was probably down to stress and too much work. After a long, leisurely breakfast he took the short drive into Police HQ. Stammers was already there and had been busy.

"Afternoon, Sarge!" he grinned.

"Fuck off Stammers, get me a large coffee will you?" Stammers laughed. "Will do Sarge, the search reports are on your desk."

Hinds leafed through the reports. Nothing. The search

teams were out again today, hopefully they would pick up something this time. Another report on his desk detailed complaints from a couple of local farmers about missing livestock . As there was so little to go on, Hinds was loathe to discount anything, so he put that report aside for later investigation. Stammers returned with a coffee.

"Here you go Sarge - oh the Chief Super said she wanted to see you. She didn't look happy."

"When does she ever?"

Hinds carried his coffee down the corridor into the lift, elbowing the button for the top floor. The lift pinged on arrival and, as the doors opened, there was a smartly dressed man looking at his fob watch. Hinds put him at mid-fifties, very well groomed, short dark hair. The man smiled, though the smile didn't reach his eyes, Hinds noticed.

"Ah, Detective Sergeant Hinds, I believe?"

Hinds exited the lift and the man got in.

"Yes - I don't believe I know your name, sir?"

"No," the stranger replied, "I don't believe you do."

The lift doors closed leaving a slightly confused Hinds in the corridor. He walked down to the big office, nodding to Pru, her receptionist.

"Go straight in, she's expecting you," she smiled

Hinds walked into the large office. Chief Superintendent Rowland stood with her back to the door, looking out over Ipswich spread below.

"Morning Ma'am."

Rowland turned; she was a stern looking woman, known as a tough but fair boss.

"Thanks for coming in, Marcus. I'll get straight to the point." She indicated a chair and sat down herself.

"The Dunwich case - we are wrapping it up."

"Wrapping it up, Ma'am? We've got someone then?"

"No, we haven't. Far from it. But we are wrapping up the investigation nonetheless. I'll need all the paperwork to pass on; the investigating staff will be re-assigned to other cases."

Hinds ran a hand over his face. "I don't understand - we've had two murders and reports in today of livestock vanishing in the area. As we speak, there's search teams going over the marshes!"

"I know, Marcus, I don't like it any more than you do. But this has come down from on-high. And I mean on-high!"

"Ah, that guy who was just here? I should've known, he had green slime written all over him. Who is he, MI5? Or worse?"

"Never you mind. Listen, get straight onto uniform, pull everyone off the case and wrap things up. If it makes you feel any better, you can put a written complaint in, I'll pass it on - though I can tell you nothing will come of it. Honestly Marcus, just leave it. Walk away!"

"And the victims? What about them?"

"Nothing will bring them back and I am assured there will be a full investigation from... well, from security agencies."

Hinds thought back to Lange's speech. He supposed that was why the doctor was so open with him - he knew damn well that Hinds could do nothing about any of it.

"Marcus - I know that look! Leave it, that's an order! Take a few days off, have a break, come back refreshed. There's plenty of other cases to be working on. Clear?"

"Crystal. I'll get onto it right away"

Hinds got up and left, leaving the Chief Superintendent tapping her pen angrily on her blotter.

An hour later, Hinds was back at Dunwich, enjoying lunch with Suzy at The Ship Inn. Over the mushroom starter, he recounted his experience at The Facility. She, in turn, passed on all the information that Bob had told her the previous night. They were both quiet during the main course, turning the ramifications of recent events over in their minds.

"So what now?" Suzy asked as coffee was served.

"What now is what my boss says. We wrap things up and move on. I've already recalled the search teams. Uniform are just tidying up, they will all be gone by the end of the day. HQ will put out a bullshit press statement."

"Just like that? Two people dead and nothing? You are just giving up?"

"I don't have any choice, Suzy. I could stick around here, but what can I achieve on my own? I doubt I'll get back into The Facility again and, if I do, then what? I can't arrest someone for carrying out Government research."

"I could splash this all over the press. Government cover-up, that kind of thing? People should know what's going on!"

"But what good would it do Suze? Five minutes outrage, then people are back to talking about X Factor. The only people who'd believe it are the conspiracy nutters."

"Hey, it was one of those 'nutters' who got all this information for us!"

"Yep, fair enough, but you know what I mean." Hinds sighed heavily. "If you'll take my advice, you'll just leave it. I know it's a good story but it could bring a lot of problems. I've seen these guys before, Suze, they don't play around."

"Aww bless, Marcus, are you worried for me?" Suzy blew on her coffee and pulled a face.

Hinds chuckled. "Just a policeman's concern for a citizen - though a very attractive citizen, I have to say!"

Suzy wriggled her eyebrows and reached across the table to place her hand on Hinds'. His mobile rang.

"I'd best get this," he said, standing and moving to the door.

"Timing," Suzy muttered to herself, "one day I'll sort out my timing!"

It was Rowland, checking that Hinds had followed her orders. He confirmed that the teams were withdrawn and uniform almost finished. As he was talking, he noticed a shiny, black Land Rover pass slowly by the pub. He could see nothing through the tinted windows, but had a sense of being observed. *So the spooks have arrived*, he thought. Going back in, he pecked Suzy on the cheek and said he'd give her a call soon. Then he went and sat in his car to think out his next move.

Back in her room, Suzy called Bob to let him know the investigation had been shut down.

"Yep, that's typical. They shut it all down, the minute something looks like getting out. It's not right, people should know!"

"Yes, that's what I said, Bob, but my policeman friend advised against it. He said to leave it."

"Well he would, wouldn't he, he works for them! Though he is right - these people can be dangerous, Suzy. In any case what proof is there? Some old files? A building that no-one can get into? No, what it needs is some real proof. Video footage, photos..." he tailed off into thought.

"Bob - what are you thinking? Listen, Marcus is right, I'm going to walk away. It's too dangerous; there's still a killer on the loose. And you stay away, you hear me? Just forget it. You hear me, Bob?"

"Yep, okay, yep. I'll speak to you soon Suzy, bye."

Chapter Seven

Bob double checked the contents of his backpack before getting on his motorbike to head north. Video camera with night vision capability, a couple of torches, bivvy bag and some food and drink. On the way he stopped off at a petrol station to buy a map of the area. Grabbing a tea and sandwich at the cafe next to the garage, he made marks on the map corresponding to the murders and The Facility. Satisfied, he continued on, arriving at Dunwich Heath just as the sun was setting. He paused to take in the view, Sellafield to the south, dim on the horizon, the setting sun lighting the heath in a rosy glow. Checking the map, he set off down a small track.

The bike was designed for off-roading and, in any case, the terrain was pretty flat. Bob moved in a circular pattern, starting close to the centre of the heath, then gradually expanding out. His last pass brought him fairly close to Dunwich, so that when the undergrowth thinned out he could see the lights of the houses on the main street.

He switched off the motorbike engine and glided to a halt, planning to take a break and set up camp in a nearby copse. He wheeled the bike into the trees and put its onto the stand, easing the pack off his shoulders. It was as he sat taking a drink from his water bottle that he heard the movement. A shuffling and rustling to his left. Bob froze. Could it be a badger or some other animal, he wondered?

His question was answered when a large, man-like shape came into view. From his position, Bob could see it silhouetted against the lights from the village. It wore a large, old overcoat and was hunched on all fours, like some huge black hound. Its head moved from side to side as though sniffing something out. Bob could see no real features but the face was pale and the eyes had a lumescent glow about them.

Bob was convinced the thing would hear his heartbeat, pounding as it was. Then it stood - it was tall, very tall! Bob shrank back into the undergrowth as the thing moved past him, cutting through the waist high ferns. Bob let it get a short lead then, treading ever so slow and careful, followed. As he went, Bob pulled his mobile from his pocket. Checking it was set to silent, he sent a text to Suzy; *AM IN DUNWICH, FOLLOWING KILLER, HEADING FOR BEACH.*

At The Ship Inn Suzy had just finished her evening meal and was in her room packing when the text came through.

"Shit!" She read the message then immediately rang Marcus.

"It's me - listen, our conspiracy guy Bob has turned up in Dunwich. Worse than that, he says he's found the killer and is following him. He's heading for the beach."

"Okay, listen, stay where you are, lock the door, I'll get up there as fast as I can. I'm not far away; I've been sat here parked near The Facility."

"What are you doing there?"

"I don't know, I've got all these ideas running through my head. In any case, sit tight, I'm on the way, stay put!"

Suzy put the phone down and sat on the bed. She thought for a few minutes then picked up her camera, pulled on her boots and coat and left the room.

He moves through the ferns, feeling strong and powerful, sated on animal flesh. He is drawn back again to the sea, the images of that other time growing stronger. They help him forget the things that happened in the Bad Place. Ahead there are lights from roads and buildings. He turns north, moving away from the lights, then turns again towards the sea, sniffing the breeze as he goes. There is nothing in the sky tonight, no

*noisy things and no flashing lights in the lanes. All is still, no
sounds except the distant whisper of sea caressing beach.*

*He crosses the short area of marsh, goes over the bank and
there it is - the calm, cold water. The moon is just rising casting
a beam of light that he imagines he could walk on... walk out
across the water to the cold bright moon.... away from them....
he could take Other with him, they could both escape. He
hunkers down on his haunches in order to show the scene to
Other. As he does there is a sound behind him - a crunch, then a
quiet word.*

Bob found it easy to trail the man through the ferns. The
marsh land proved more difficult, but luckily he could see
exactly where the creature was headed, across the marsh and
up the bank. He gave it a short lead, then followed. It was
hard to move quietly through the sucking mud, he ended up
half sprawled most of the time. Eventually, he reached the
firmness of the bank and, keeping low, climbed over it. He
could see the thing ahead, squatted close to the sea, bathed in
moonlight. Bob paused to send another text to Suzy; *AM ON
BEACH JUST NORTH OF VILLAGE.*

As he went to put the phone away his hand slipped and the
phone tumbled out of his grip. He lurched forward to catch it
and ended up going headfirst down the bank, landing in an
untidy heap on the pebbles. Before he could stop himself, he
swore.

Looking up he could see the creature had turned to look
over his shoulder at him. Bob gulped and, forgetting all about
the phone, got to his feet and began to run towards the
village. With an hoarse cry the squatting figure leapt to its
feet. Over the sound of his own flight, Bob could hear the
shingle crunching behind him. Fear spurred him on, his arms

pumping at his sides, breath coming in great, ragged gasps. He dare not look back. Suddenly there was a light up ahead - a torch! It was Suzy; she waved at him and shouted.

Suzy shone the light at Bob as he ran towards her. Then the torch beam played past Bob and she saw what followed.

At its full height, it must have been seven feet tall. Its gait was contorted and awkward. Its face was pale, eyes blazing, and its mouth was stretched wide open. A wild tuft of red hair stood up from the thing's scalp. Its arms were spread wide; the fingers ended in curved talons. The thing wore a large old overcoat, which opened up and out as it ran, spreading like wings, giving the appearance of some twisted angel. The upper torso was hairless, with pale, yellowish skin. The ribs were prominent, the chest rising and falling. But as the torch played over the creature, Suzy could see its whole body.

Its lower half was covered in coarse black hair. A frond of writhing tentacles formed a belt around the waist, pulsing with garish colours as the thing breathed . With horrifying clarity Suzy noticed what appeared to be eyes studded across the thing's lower torso and upper thighs. The legs terminated in saurian-like feet, three large toes splayed out into the pebbles.

Suzy froze; even the scream froze in her throat. Her brain struggled to find some sense in what she was seeing. With a lurch, the thing moved closer to Bob. Flinging out an arm, it caught him a blow on the back of his shoulder. Bob went hurtling forward, hitting the ground hard, his arm twisted at an odd angle beneath him.

The three froze in a moonlit tableau. Bob gasping on the floor, face contorted in pain. The thing stood over him, jaws gaping. Suzy, holding the torch in numb fingers. It was Suzy who moved first. From some depths of her being a shout erupted. "Leave him alone! Back off, leave him alone!"

The thing snarled and turned towards her, raising a hand to strike. Then it stopped. It tilted its face to one side, examining Suzy closely. The jaws closed, the strike never came. Instead, the hand moved out slowly, to touch Suzy's hair. Then the thing slowly sank back on its haunches, seemingly in a trance, its eyes rolled back in their sockets.

Suzy wasted no time in analysing the situation. Helping Bob to his feet, she set off back down the beach as fast as they could go. She saw headlights sweeping into the car park. Quickly she helped Bob get over the low bank and into the car park, where Marcus was just jumping out of the car.

"Are you okay? Is the killer here?"

"Behind us!" gasped Suzy. She noticed Marcus had a crowbar in his hand.

"Alright get back, get into the car and lock the doors!"

Suzy assisted Bob to the car; he was holding his arm and moaning. "Come on Bob, stay with me." Putting him in the rear seat, she turned back toward Marcus. He stood poised, crowbar held aloft, breath steaming in the night air. All was quiet. Suzy moved to his side, still breathing hard.

He is confused. The running man is obviously of them, someone to be hurt and to be food. But the other one - she was like the one in his memory.... him, Other and the man and woman. He cannot remember faces, but remembers blue sky, yellow sun, red hair, laughter and happiness. Squatting, he speaks to Other, sharing what has just happened. Other is roaring in delight. He seems stronger somehow; there is a man's face, screaming, then a feeding; not just the blood and flesh, but the life force. Other feels powerful and gorged. KILL! he screams, KILL! He stands again. Other is right. Them must

195

all die! Them only bring pain! He leaps to his feet and bounds
ahead over the small bank. A man stands there, with the female
behind him. The man has an arm raised and is holding
something as if to hurt him.

With a sudden snarl the thing appeared at the top of the
bank. It sprang at Marcus, who swung the crowbar with all
his strength. The bar bounced of the creature's arm and
Marcus was knocked flying by a buffeting strike. Suzy
screamed. The thing looked to her and to Marcus, as if
deciding which to attack first.

There was a sudden squeal of tyres and a blinding white
light spotlighted the creature. It flung its arm up to cover its
face. Marcus, lying dazed on the ground, was vaguely aware of
shouting and running boots around him.

"Fire, man, fire!" a voice shouted and the night was rent
asunder by a huge tongue of flame that caught the
creature square on. The air was filled with a chemical smell,
followed by the stench of burning flesh. The creature writhed
and tried to escape, but the man with the flamethrower was
relentless. The creature wheeled and fell to its knees. Its
features became distorted and melted under the merciless
flame. It flung its arms to the sky, lifted its face and roared
"OTHER!!! HELP MEEEE!!!"

Within a minute it was little more than a shrivelled hulk,
but still the flame kept coming. Marcus and Suzy retched as
they were engulfed in a noxious cloud.

"Team Alpha, secure the car park! Team Bravo, I want this
whole area cordoned off to a thousand yards, no one in or
out! Bradshaw, cease fire!" The voice shouted again.

Marcus held Suzy close and they moved towards the black
Land Rover. Hendry was there, it was he who had been

barking the orders. Around them, dark clad men, all armed, were a hive of activity.

"Are you harmed?" Hendry asked.

"No, we're okay," Marcus replied, recognising the man from the lift at HQ. "I took a bit of a whack but I'll be alright."

"And you, Miss Hodges?"

"Yes, I'm fine, but who are you and how-"

"Who we are is not important, as to how, well we were monitoring your mobile communications."

"What? But you can't do that, that's illegal!" Suzy protested.

"Suzy - they can do that." Marcus suggested quietly.

"And where is this Bob character?" asked Hendry, casting his gaze around. Suzy glanced towards Marcus' car. Bob must have tucked himself down in the back seat.

"Bob didn't make it, the thing got him further up the beach."

"Alright. Now, listen up! You didn't see anything, you didn't hear anything and you will remember nothing about this! You will tell no-one, you will write nothing, you will never speak of what happened here, do you understand?"

"But that thing...what was it? And I'm a reporter, I'll write what I bloody well like, you can't stop me!" Suzy insisted.

"I'm afraid he can," said Marcus.

"Precisely, Miss Hodges, listen to your friend. Not only could I stop anything you write from being printed, I could also see to it that you disappeared - both of you! So all in all, I'd say you were bloody lucky to be walking away from this as you are! If you are still here in thirty seconds, I'll have you shot as terrorists - do I make myself clear?"

Suzy went to protest further, but Marcus grabbed her arm.

"Come on, let's get out of here." He steered her to the car and they got in.

"You ok Bob?" whispered Marcus without turning round.

"No, my arm hurts like fuck," came the quiet reply, "but I got some good footage on the camcorder!"

Suzy laughed, easing the tension. "Good lad. Let's go."

The car swung out of the car park, two of the armed men moving aside to let them through.

"I'll drop you at the pub to pick up your car, Suzy, then get Bob to hospital. Maybe later we can have a look at that footage?" Marcus suggested.

"It's not right that he threatened us, "compained Suzy.

"It isn't right and it isn't fair," said Marcus, "but we can be thankful that it's all over now!"

Epilogue

Lange had just returned to his office when a call from security took him rushing back to the monitor room. Subject E had become highly agitated, flailing around the room, smashing into the blood-streaked walls. The creature also appeared to have grown. As Lange watched, it paused, then the face abruptly wheeled to stare into the camera, directly at him, he felt. His skin crawled; even he found it difficult to hold that unearthly gaze. The thing froze for a moment, it's eyes rolling back into their sockets. Then, with startling speed, it suddenly moved towards the chamber exit. There was a dull clang as its bulk hit the door.

"What is it doing? Could it be trying to escape?" Lange breathed." But why? Why now?"

He sat, puzzled as the thing smashed its bulk against the room's exit. Realisation hit him in the pit of his stomach.

"Of course... they are twins! The psychic link! If one is hurt, the other will feel its pain! " He span to the security guard.

"Get me Hendry, quickly!"

Other feels powerful following its feeding. Now anger swells its power, as it thought-senses danger. There is a sudden jolt and it becomes overwhelmed with a burning sensation, as though every atom of its being is aflame! The pain inspires it to greater rage, the corpulent, bloated body writhes, but the agony gives it strength!

Outside, the security team run to the Airlock. They hear an unearthly howling from within, then a sudden boom. A rhythmic pounding begins deep inside the building. After a few moments, the noise stops. The guards look nervously at each other; one turns and runs. The remaining pair jump at another large slam, this time against the outer door!

It is followed by another and they watch, gripped by a terrible anticipation, as a large dent develops in the heavy steel. Boom! Boom! More hits, more dents.

Slowly, inevitably, a gap appears, then widens in the edge of the Airlock. There is a sudden, pregnant silence. The guards stand transfixed, hands clutching each others arms.

With a scuttling, scratching movement, a long, thin, multi-jointed limb emerges through the gap. At that sight, the guards break and flee. They are not there to witness the several more spindly limbs that sprout from the gap, followed by a pulsing tentacle that grips the edge of the Airlock.

With a final agonised scream of metal, the outer door is wrenched wide open. And then all Hell breaks loose.....

To be continued in 'The Dunwich Legacy'.

If you have enjoyed this book,
please leave a review on
Amazon. Thanks!

www.innsmouthgold.com

Lightning Source UK Ltd.
Milton Keynes UK
UKHW040650301018
331393UK00019B/364/P